Back by Popular Demand

A collector's edition of favorite titles
from one of the world's best-loved
romance authors. Harlequin is proud to
bring back these sought after titles and
present them as one cherished collection.

BETTY NEELS: COLLECTOR'S EDITION

A GEM OF A GIRL
WISH WITH THE CANDLES
COBWEB MORNING
HENRIETTA'S OWN CASTLE
CASSANDRA BY CHANCE
VICTORY FOR VICTORIA
SISTER PETERS IN AMSTERDAM
THE MAGIC OF LIVING
SATURDAY'S CHILD
FATE IS REMARKABLE
A STAR LOOKS DOWN
HEAVEN IS GENTLE

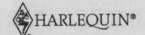

HARLEQUIN®

Betty Neels spent her childhood and youth in Devonshire before training as a nurse and midwife. She was an army nursing sister during the war, married a Dutchman, and subsequently lived in Holland for fourteen years. She now lives with her husband in Dorset, and has a daughter and grandson. Her hobbies are reading, animals, old buildings and, of course, writing. Betty started to write on retirement from nursing, incited by a lady in a library bemoaning the lack of romantic novels.

Mrs. Neels is always delighted to receive fan letters, but would truly appreciate it if they could be directed to Harlequin Mills & Boon Ltd., 18-24 Paradise Road, Richmond, Surrey, TW9 1SR, England.

Books by Betty Neels

BETTY NEELS
COBWEB MORNING

COLLECTOR'S EDITION

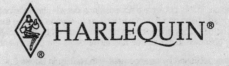
HARLEQUIN®

TORONTO • NEW YORK • LONDON
AMSTERDAM • PARIS • SYDNEY • HAMBURG
STOCKHOLM • ATHENS • TOKYO • MILAN • MADRID
PRAGUE • WARSAW • BUDAPEST • AUCKLAND

ISBN 0-373-83388-1

COBWEB MORNING

First North American Publication 1976.

Copyright © 1975 by Betty Neels.

Printed in U.S.A.

CHAPTER ONE

THE hospital dining-room was almost empty save for the maid on duty, wiping down tables in a belligerent manner and in an ever-increasing circle around the one occupied table, whose three occupants watched her warily between their mouthfuls of the wholesome if unimaginative fish pie which had been all that was left on the day's menu. She returned their looks with a cross one of her own and spoke sourly.

'There ain't no afters, it'll 'ave ter be cheese and biscuits.'

The eldest of the three ladies, a thin person in her forties with an ill-tempered face and wearing a ward Sister's uniform, merely frowned, while the small, pretty creature sitting opposite her, also in Sister's uniform but looking somehow unaccustomed to it, looked apologetically at the speaker and murmured that it didn't matter. It was left to the third member of the party to turn a pair of fine eyes in the maid's direction and request her in a crisp voice to bring the cheese and biscuits. 'And I have no doubt,' she went on in her pleasant voice, 'that you can find us a pot of tea, can't you, Bertha?'

She smiled with such charm that the grumpy Bertha smiled back, flung down her cloth, and although muttering, went away to fetch what had been requested of her, while the Sister who had spoken sat back in her chair and began a desultory conversation with her two companions. She was a very pretty young woman, with a creamy skin and abundant hair, as dark as her eyes, and with a delightful nose which tilted ever so slightly at its tip above a generously curved mouth and a small determined chin. She was a tall, well built girl, whose figure showed off to perfection the uniform she was wearing—that of a hospital Sister, too, but rather different from the others, and decidedly better fitting, moreover, the neat coil of hair above her neck was crowned with the frilled and goffered cap of one of the famous London hospitals, its strings tied in a bow under her chin; a piece of old-fashioned nonsense which vastly became her.

The cheese and biscuits and a large pot of tea arrived, were consumed hurriedly, and the three ladies prepared to leave. It was already two o'clock as they rose from the table and the November afternoon had dwindled into a wet, grey prospect which promised an even worse evening. Alexandra

Dobbs twitched her bows into a more comfortable position with a well-kept hand and looked out of the window as they crossed the large, comfortless room. There was nothing to see outside; a hotchpotch of walls and annexes and a few trees beyond; she would have liked to have been back at her own hospital, with the traffic thundering past in a subdued roar and the prospect of a pleasant evening in the Sister's sitting-room when she went off duty, or what was more likely, a meal out with one of the Medical Registrars, Anthony Ferris—a young man who, at thirty, was climbing up his particular ladder successfully enough and had lately given her to believe that he would like her to climb with him. Indeed, she had wondered once or twice in the last few days if she would decide to marry him; she had, since the age of seventeen—ten years ago—been the recipient of a number of proposals of marriage, and while refusing them politely, had taken none of them seriously, but Anthony was different; he was ambitious, he wanted a consulting practice, a good income and a suitable wife. The only reason that she hadn't encouraged him so far was because she had a niggling feeling that she wasn't suitable. Besides, when she really thought seriously about it, she wasn't sure that she wanted to marry him; she had told herself that it was silly to indulge in child-

ish fancies, Anthony and she were well suited—
everyone who knew them told her that—and yet she
had the oddest feeling that somewhere in the world
there was a man waiting for her—a man about
whom she would have no doubts at all.

This nebulous figure was at the back of her mind
now, as she walked back with her companions to
the new Intensive Care Unit, recently opened at the
hospital—a small unit of two beds, for the hospital
was small, too; serving a provincial town and its
surrounding rural west country area. It was this unit
which was the reason for her being there; she had
been Sister-in-Charge of the large, always busy unit
at St Job's for several years now, and had been
seconded to the hospital in order to instruct its staff:
Sister Baxter, who had no wish to be trained, anyway, not because she didn't want to run the new
unit, but because she considered that no one could
instruct her about anything; she knew it already,
and Sister Pim, very young and inexperienced and
quite frankly terrified of Sister Baxter. A fine set-
up, Alexandra considered as she went over the apparatus just once more. It was the third day of her
visit and she was due back in the morning; it was
a pity, without wishing anyone any harm, that a
patient needing intensive care couldn't be admitted,
so that she could judge for herself if Sister Baxter

knew what she was about. She very much doubted it, and Sister Pim, although a charming girl, had had no experience at all; she had barely qualified when she had been offered the post. On her own she might do very well, but with Sister Baxter bullying her she would turn into a yes-woman, doing what she was told whether it was right or not.

A pity, mused Alexandra, who had never been a yes-woman in her life, partly because she had an elder brother and two younger ones, all of whom had made it their business to see that she could stand up for herself. Her mother, watching her lovely little daughter climbing trees, swimming like a fish and giving as good as she got when it came to holding her own against her brothers, had at times worried that she might grow up a tomboy, but Alexandra hadn't; she had become a charming girl with nice manners, a willingness to help at church bazaars and other rural events, a pleasant way with children, and an endless patience with the elderly and their foibles. The perfect wife, Mrs Dobbs had told herself, well satisfied, and had spent the next eight or nine years wondering why Alexandra didn't get married. Instead the dear girl had carved a career for herself in the nursing profession and had shown no signs of wanting to marry at all, although just lately Mrs Dobbs had been more hopeful; Alexandra had mentioned, more and more frequently, Anthony Ferris. Mrs Dobbs, an incurable romantic, allowed herself to plan a wedding outfit, but took great care to keep her hopes to herself.

The short afternoon slid into dusk and then dark. Sister Baxter went to her tea, taking the meek little Lucy Pim with her, and Alexandra, due off duty when they returned, set about making a final check before she left. She still had to see the Senior Nursing Officer, but that wouldn't take long—she would pack that evening, she told herself contentedly, and catch an early morning train back to London.

The other two had returned, and she was on the point of leaving them when there was the sound of a car, driven hard and braking to a halt outside the hospital entrance. It was followed, after the shortest possible interval, by the sound of footsteps coming down the corridor towards them, and an imperative voice issuing instructions. Alexandra, hearing it, felt a pang of sympathy for the elderly porter on duty—he liked to do things in his own time and it was obvious that just for once, he wasn't being given that chance.

The owner of the voice appeared seconds later, an immensely tall man and powerfully built, making light of the burden he was carrying—an unconscious girl. He paused momentarily as he entered and asked without preamble: 'Who's in charge here?'

Sister Baxter, bristling with authority, answered him. 'I am, but this isn't the Casualty Department; there isn't one at this hospital, you must go to...'

She wasn't given the chance to finish; the man had laid the girl down gently on a couch and was bending over her. 'I know, I know,' he said impatiently, 'but this girl's been in a car crash and she needs to go on to a ventilator at once. I've no intention of travelling another five or six miles to have the Casualty Officer tell me that she will have to be brought back here for treatment. Kindly summon the officer on duty and give me a hand.' He added as an afterthought: 'I'm a doctor.'

He lifted his head and looked at Sister Baxter with scarcely concealed impatience, his blue eyes passing from her to Sister Pim and thence to Alexandra. He was a handsome man, in his thirties, with a straight nose and a mobile mouth. His hair, now grizzled, must have been very fair when he was younger. Alexandra noted these things as she stepped forward; it wasn't her department and she wasn't in charge, but Sister Baxter was being tiresome and little Lucy Pim was, for the moment, unable to cope. She said calmly: 'Would you prefer the Cape? The Bird's is here if it's only for a short time—is she very bad?' She turned her head and spoke to Lucy, ignoring Sister Baxter's outraged face. 'Will you get Mr Collins? He's on duty, I believe.'

She was competent at her work; she and the strange doctor had the Cape ventilator going by the time Mr Collins and Sister Pim arrived, and within a few minutes, after they had prepared the girl for examination, the two men set to work. Alexandra had been surprised that Mr Collins had raised no objection to the strange doctor's obvious assumption that he should take charge of the case, it was really quite unethical, but he had murmured something with a good deal of respect when the stranger had introduced himself, so briefly and softly that she, to her annoyance, had been unable to hear a word of it. But there was no time to speculate about anyone else but the patient for the moment, for she was in a bad way.

She was young—eighteen or nineteen, perhaps, and very pretty, although the prettiness was marred now by her ashen face and blood-matted hair. A fractured base of skull, probably, and they would have to work hard to pull her round, although the ventilator was proving its worth already, virtually breathing for her until such time as she would—it was to be hoped—take over for herself once more.

The two men muttered together, making their slow, careful examination, and Alexandra, with a moment to spare, took a look around her. Sister Baxter was glowering from behind one of the emergency trolleys, later on, when everything had settled down once more there would probably be a dust-up. Alexandra tried a smile and got a lowering look in return. Lucy Pim, over the first shock of finding herself actually working the various apparatus Alexandra had been so painstakingly teaching her for the last day or so, was proving herself very useful; she would be all right, after all.

Alexandra heaved a sigh of relief and then swallowed it as her eye lighted on the seventh person in the department; a thin, angular lady, no longer young, with a sharp, pointed nose and iron grey hair drawn back into a small bun under what Alexandra could only describe to herself as a lady's hat. Its wearer, moreover, was clad in a sensible teed suit, and her feet were shod with equally sensible lace-up shoes. A hint of pearls at the lady's throat and the gloves and handbag, leather but a little shabby, gave her a possible clue. Someone's aunt; the very counterpart of aunts of her own, and probably thousands more. The girl's? She would have to be asked presently, but in the meantime she was behaving with commendable calm and not getting in the way even though she shouldn't be there in the first place. She caught her eye and they exchanged smiles as she handed the strange doctor an X-ray form just a second before he could open his mouth to ask for one.

Sister Pim had sped away with it, with instructions to bring back the porters with her when he turned his eyes, very cool, on Alexandra. 'And what are you doing here?' he wanted to know. 'Isn't that a St Job's cap—'

She eyed him with a similar coolness, not liking his tone. 'I'm here to get this unit started,' she told him briefly. He wasn't English; he spoke it perfectly, but there was something in his deep voice…she would find out later, meanwhile: 'The lady by the door,' she prompted him. 'Is she the mother? If so, she shouldn't be here—if you would speak to her, I'll take her along to the waiting room.'

His smile was so unexpected that she caught her breath. 'My aunt,' he said, 'Miss Euphemia Thrums, a formidable lady and of great help to me when this accident occurred. She insisted upon coming with me and I didn't care to leave her alone.' His voice was blandly authoritative.

'Oh,' said Alexandra, rather at a loss, and then: 'Were there any relations or friends…the police…?'

'Are already dealing with it,' he told her smoothly. 'The girl was driving herself—presumably there would be papers in her handbag or the car.'

It was time for Alexandra to take her observations again; she bent to her task and was just finished when the porters arrived with the portable X-ray machine, which left her with nothing much to do for a few minutes; Sister Pim was managing very nicely, so Alexandra drifted quietly back to where Sister Baxter was still standing and encountered a look from that lady which would have reduced anyone of a less sturdy nature than hers to pulp.

'This is highly irregular,' began Sister Baxter. 'If anything is said, I shall hold you personally responsible.' She nodded towards the lady by the door. 'And who is she, I should like to know, and this man, ordering us about...'

'He's a doctor,' Alexandra pointed out, 'they do order people about when it's necessary, you know. After all, they're the ones who know.'

'Yes, but who is he?'

Alexandra studied the man. He had an air of authority, but his clothes, though well cut, were a little shabby; there was nothing about him to denote the successful physician or famous surgeon. Her speculations were interrupted by the entry of the hospital's senior anaesthetist, Doctor White, who added to the mystery by greeting the stranger as an old friend and shaking hands. What was more, he crossed the room to shake hands with Miss Thrums too, although he didn't stop to talk to her, returning to the couch where the radiographer had done his work and was on the point of leaving. The three doctors went with him, the stranger pausing to lift a beckoning finger at Alexandra, and when she reached his side: 'You will be good enough to remain with the patient,' he said, 'and let us know at once if you have reason for alarm.' He nodded, staring at her as though he didn't like her at all, and followed the others out.

Alexandra, checking this and that and making neat entries on the chart, ruminated with the tiny piece of her brain not occupied with her work, that her evening plans had been squashed: it was already an hour after she should have been off duty and she saw no chance of getting away for quite some time; it would have to be decided where the girl was to go, there would be delays while her relations were sent for, another hour, she reckoned before the doctors would make their decisions, and once they had, she vowed silently, she would hand over to the other two Sisters and streak off to her room and pack.

She looked up and caught Miss Thrums' eyes on her and exclaimed with sudden contrition: 'Oh, you poor thing—Sister Pim, do you suppose we could charm someone into giving Miss Thrums a cup of tea, she must need one after the nasty time she's had.'

She was on the point of suggesting that she might like to go to the waiting room down the passage, too, when she remembered that the doctor had brought her with him and would probably turn nasty if she took it upon herself to send his aunt away, however kindly she meant it.

Miss Thrums smiled tiredly. 'That would be delightful.' She spoke in a whisper, with due regard for her surroundings, all the same she had a carrying voice. 'What a very efficient girl you are, Sister—St Job's, are you not? Miss Trott is a friend of mine.' Miss Trott was the Principal Nursing Officer and rather an old duck. The doctor's aunt went on: 'I hope that poor girl will be all right—we were directly behind her, you know, so fortunate, because Taro was able to give help within seconds.'

She broke off as Sister Pim came back with the tea, and settled back to enjoy it as the men came back. It was Mr White who crossed the room to speak to Alexandra. 'I believe that you are due back at St Job's tomorrow, Sister Dobbs? We are hoping that you will co-operate with us in the plan we have decided upon. The patient has a fractured base—she's very ill, but provided we can get specialist treatment for her within a reasonable time, I think we may hope for complete recovery. I've been in touch with Mr Thrush—you know him, of course, and he is willing to accept her as a patient of St Job's. Now, would you be willing to escort her on the journey—ambulance, of course, and not immediately—possibly in a few hours' time, by then we should get a very good idea of her condition and be reasonably certain that she can stand the journey. You will have everything laid on, needless to say.'

She liked Mr White, he was elderly and balding and kind, and reminded her of her own father. She agreed at once and he looked relieved, and when she looked across at the stranger, she saw, not relief on his handsome features, but satisfaction—so it was he who had been behind their scheme, she decided shrewdly. She asked on impulse: 'Could I have this doctor's name, sir? We shall need it for the report.'

She hadn't spoken loudly, yet before Mr White could answer, the subject of her question was crossing the room to join them. 'You agree to what we ask?' he wanted to know, and when she nodded: 'My name is van Dresselhuys, you will need it for your report, no doubt.'

'Thank you. Mine's Dobbs.' She gave him a little nod, said 'Excuse me,' smiled brilliantly at Doctor White and went back to where Sister Pim was busy with the patient.

The ambulance left four hours later with Alexandra, her packing done in a swift ten minutes or so, in attendance. The stranger and his aunt had disappeared; vaguely, at the back of her busy mind, she was disappointed at this, but there really was no time to indulge in her own thoughts. She supervised the transfer of the girl to the ambulance, and collected the charts and notes from Lucy, who had volunteered to stay on duty until they went. No one had inquired about the girl; the police had drawn a blank and there was nothing in her handbag to give them any clue as to her identity; there was no driving licence there either and the car, a write-off, had borne a Midlands number-plate. Their search for her identity might take some time. Alexandra, hearing this, gave a resigned shrug and went out to the ambulance, primed with Mr White's instructions for the journey.

There was a Morris 1000 drawn up beside it, in

it sat Miss Thrums, and bending over its open, mid-dle-aged bonnet was the strange doctor. He took no notice of Alexandra; it was his aunt who thrust her head out of the car window and said cheerfully: 'We are accompanying you, Sister—we have to go to London in any case, and my nephew is anxious that the girl should have every care.'

Alexandra bristled. 'Perhaps he would prefer to travel in the ambulance?' she asked with dangerous sweetness.

The doctor answered this for himself, without bothering to take his head from under the bonnet. 'My dear good woman, why on earth should I wish to do that when you are perfectly competent to at-tend to the patient? We shall travel behind you, and if you need my help you have only to signal me.'

'Just as you wish,' said Alexandra, still very sweet, 'and be so good as not to address me as your good woman.'

She turned her back on his deep chuckle and flounced into the ambulance.

It was a great pity that she had to stop the am-bulance twice during the journey and ask for his help; something which he gave with a calm des-patch which she was forced to admit was all that she could have asked for. On the second occasion they were delayed for half an hour, working over their patient in the confines of the ambulance, with the ambulance men hovering, helpful and resourceful, at their backs, and when at last the doctor pronounced it safe to continue their journey, he added a rider to the effect that they should make the best speed they could. Luckily they were on the outskirts of Woking by now and at two o'clock in the morning the roads were fairly clear. They arrived at St Job's without further alarms and the patient was taken at once to the Intensive Care Unit, with Alexandra, her eyes very bright in her tired face, accompanying her. She hadn't stopped to speak to the doctor; the all-important thing was to get the girl back on to the ventilator again and she heaved a sigh of relief at being back in her own department once more with two night nurses waiting and everything to hand. The girl responded fairly quickly, and once she was sure of that Alexandra gave her report to the Night Sister, repeated it to the Registrar and yawning widely, started off for the Nurses' Home. She hadn't seen any more of the doctor and she didn't expect to; probably he would see Mr Thrush's registrar and then continue his journey.

She went sleepily down the stairs and found him at the bottom, deep in conversation with the Casualty Officer on duty, but as she reached them, he bade the young man good-bye, took her by the arm and led her through the front hall and down the main corridor, opening a door half way down it and pushing her gently inside.

'I can't go in here,' Alexandra, now very much awake, pointed out, 'this is the consultants' room.'

'I know, but they aren't here at this time of night—only Aunty. The Night Super sent some coffee down for us and I promised her that I would see that you had a cup before you went to bed.'

Miss Thrums was sitting at the large table in the centre of the room, very upright and looking as though staying up all night in awkward circumstances was something she was quite accustomed to. She nodded bracingly at Alexandra, begged her to take a seat and poured her some coffee.

'A trying evening,' she observed. 'I can only trust that the girl will recover.'

Alexandra murmured, because the doctor had nothing to say, and then asked: 'Have you somewhere to go for the rest of the night? I could get Night Super to let you have the rooms we keep for relations—you could at least have rest...'

This time the doctor spoke. 'Very kind, Sister Dobbs, but we have been offered beds at Mr Thrush's.' His tone implied that it really was no business of hers, and if she hadn't been so tired, she might have felt inclined to take him up on that, instead she drank her coffee, said good-bye to Miss Thrums, and taking a brisk farewell of the doctor, started for the door to find him with her as she reached it.

'You have been very kind,' he told her, 'I'm grateful. Let us hope that the patient repays you by recovering.'

'Yes,' said Alexandra, vague with tiredness, 'and I hope they find her family soon, too.' She knitted her brows, trying to think of something else to say by way of a pleasant farewell and he smiled a little. 'You're asleep on your feet. Goodnight, Miss Dobbs.'

It was as she was tumbling into bed that she remembered that he hadn't said good-bye, only goodnight.

CHAPTER TWO

I⊤ had been a very short night; Alexandra got up and dressed with the greatest reluctance and went down to join her friends at breakfast, a meal eaten in a hurry, although she still found time to answer the questions put to her.

'And what's this I hear,' asked Ruth Page, Women's Surgical Sister, 'about you arriving in the small hours with a tall dark stranger? I met Meg coming off night duty and she was full of him—driving a Rolls, I suppose...'

'As a matter of fact,' said Alexandra, 'his hair's grizzled and he was driving a Morris 1000. Oh, and his aunt was with him.' When the shrieks of laughter had died down, she added demurely: 'It went like a bomb.'

'Yes, but what about him?' persisted Ruth. 'What's his name—how old is he—did he turn you on?'

Alexandra considered. 'His name's van Dresselhuys, that's Dutch, isn't it—though his English was perfect. I've no idea how old he would be and I thought him rather rude and bad-tempered, though,' she added fairly, 'he was pretty super when the girl had a cardiac arrest.' She swallowed the last of her tea and got to her feet. 'I'd better be on my way, I suppose; there's a long list and if she's fit enough they'll want to operate, though heaven knows where they'll fit her in.'

Several of her companions got up too and as they walked through the hospital to their various wards, someone asked: 'This girl—who is she?'

'That's just it, no one knows yet. She hadn't any papers or anything with her, the car was hired from a garage in the Midlands—Wolverhampton, I believe, and until the police can trace her family or friends she can't be identified.'

'It's to be hoped that she'll be able to tell us herself before long,' Ruth spoke soberly. 'I'll get her once she's out of the ICU, I suppose?'

'I should think so—lord, there's the panic bell, someone's arresting.' Alexandra was off down the corridor like a bullet from a gun.

It was old Mr Dasher, who had been in her unit for five days already, he had been admitted a few hours before Alexandra had gone away, and here he was still, she thought worriedly, looking not one scrap better; she got to work on him and was getting a little response when Anthony Ferris arrived. It wasn't until the old man was once more breathing and she had spent a careful five minutes with the unconscious girl that she felt able to leave things in the hands of her staff nurse and go along to her office, so that she might go through the various papers and messages on her desk. And of course Anthony went with her, and when she sat down, sat down too, on the only other chair in the room.

Alexandra, short-tempered from lack of sleep and an unexplained dissatisfaction with life in general, frowned at him. 'Anthony, I've heaps of jobs to catch up on and that girl will probably be going to theatre…'

He smiled at her with a condescending tolerance which set her splendid teeth on edge and made it worse by saying: 'Poor little girl—I hear you had to put up with some foreign type, ordering you around. One of those know-alls, I suppose.'

'Then you suppose wrong.' Alexandra had forgotten the Dutchman's arrogant manner and couldn't spring fast enough to his defence. 'He was extremely civil and he knew exactly what to do— I should never have got the girl here alive if it hadn't been for him.'

Anthony was too conceited a man to be worried by her championship of someone he hadn't even met. 'My poor sweet,' he said, 'how kind of you to stick up for him…'

'If I might echo those words?' queried Doctor van Dresselhuys from the door.

She stared at him, her pretty mouth slightly open; she hadn't expected him, though she had thought of him several times, and here he was, in her office, of all places. She said, inadequately: 'Oh, hullo, I thought you'd gone.'

He leaned against the wall, dwarfing Anthony, and looking, despite his well-worn clothes, elegant. Indeed, he made the other man's rather way-out style of dressing look rather cheap. 'Er—no. Mr Thrush asked me if I would give the anaesthetic— he intends to do a decompression.'

His cool eyes flickered over Anthony, and Alexandra made haste to introduce the two men, but they had little to say to each other; after a few minutes Anthony announced, rather importantly, that he had work to do and edged to the door, saying over-loudly as he went: 'I'll see you as usual this evening, Alexandra—we might dine and dance somewhere.' At the door he turned. ''Bye, darling.'

Doctor van Dresselhuys hadn't moved, he still leant against the door, the picture of idleness, only his eyes gleamed. When Anthony had gone, he asked casually: 'Going to marry him?'

'No, I'm not!' declared Alexandra explosively. Anthony had behaved like a bad-tempered child and

she had given him no right at all to call her darling;
he'd been showing off, of course, hoping to impress
this large man, whose very largeness, she suspected,
had annoyed him, and who, unless she was very
much mistaken, was secretly amused.

He didn't say anything else, just went on looking
at her with his blue eyes until she felt the soft colour creeping into her cheeks. It deepened when he
said softly: 'You're a remarkably lovely girl.'

She disliked him, she told herself seethingly, as
much as she disliked Anthony—as much as she disliked men with a capital M. She pressed her lips
together and lifted her chin at him, and was outraged when he asked, still casually: 'Did I come at
the wrong moment—was your young man on the
point of proposing?'

'No, he was not,' she snapped, 'and even if he
were,' she went on crossly, 'I really don't see that
it's any business of yours.' She got up. 'And you
really must excuse me, I have work to do.'

'Ah, yes. I've come to see the patient, if you
would be so kind?' He stood aside to let her pass
and followed her into the unit, where he became all
at once a doctor, asking questions in a calm voice,
reading the notes, examining the girl with meticu-
lous care. There was no hidden amusement now; he
was absorbed in what he was doing, and Alexandra

was no longer a lovely girl; she was a skilled someone in a white gown, who answered his questions
with the intelligence expected of her. Finally he
nodded, thanked her and went away; she didn't see
him again for quite some time, but when the theatre
nurse came to escort the girl to theatre, she was
treated to that young lady's ecstatic opinion of him;
he had, it seemed, charmed every female he had
encountered. Alexandra was left with the feeling
that she must be lacking in something or other.

The girl came back, holding her own well, and
as far as was possible to judge at this stage, the
operation had been a success. Alexandra set to work
on her, and when Doctor van Dresselhuys came to
see the patient in Mr Thrush's company, she was
far too occupied to spare a thought for him.

Late off duty, because she had been a little anxious about her patient, Alexandra took the lift down
to ground level, nipped smartly along a succession
of passages and crossed the small ornamental garden which separated the Nurses' Home from the
hospital. It was pitch dark by now and there was
no reason why she should encounter anyone at that
hour, so that the vague feeling of disappointment
she experienced was all the more surprising. In her
room, she kicked off her shoes, removed her cap
and went along to run a bath; she met Ruth on the

way back and delayed to share a pot of tea with her. Anthony had said that he would meet her, but he hadn't said when or where; his airy remark about meeting her as usual meant nothing; they had gone out fairly frequently together, it was true, but he had implied that they went dining and dancing nightly. Frowningly, she could only remember two occasions in the last three months or so when he had taken her somewhere really decent for dinner, and never to a dance.

She accepted a second cup; let Anthony wait, better still, let him telephone over to the home and ask if she was ready.

She had bathed and was in her dressing gown doing her hair when someone shouted up the stairs that she was wanted on the telephone. She went without haste and said a grumpy 'Well?' into the receiver.

'Good lord,' Anthony's voice sounded irritable. 'What's keeping you? You've been off duty for an hour or more.'

'So I have, but not knowing where I was to meet you as usual or to which marvellous place you were taking me to dine and dance, there didn't seem much point in doing anything about it.'

She heard his embarrassed laugh. 'Look here, old girl, you must have known I only said that because that nonchalant type was standing there laughing at me. Come on now,' his voice took on a wheedling note, 'throw on a coat and we'll go out and have a meal.'

She hesitated; she had missed her supper and all she had in her room was a tin of biscuits. She said, 'All right,' and added, 'I think you were very silly,' before she put down the receiver.

He was waiting for her at the hospital entrance when she got there, ten minutes later. Because it was such a dark and damp evening, she had put on a raincoat, belted round her slim waist, and dragged on a wool cap, shrouding her dark hair, then added a matching scarf, yards long, which she wound round her neck to keep out the cold; totally unglamorous, she decided, taking a quick look at herself, but sensible.

It was a nasty quirk of fate that Doctor van Dresselhuys should have been standing in the entrance hall, talking to Mr Thrush. He looked up as she went past them, his brows arching slowly as he took deliberate stock of her, while his mouth curved into a smile, conveying plainly that her appearance hardly tallied with that of a young woman on her way to dine and dance. She scowled at him, smiled sweetly at Mr Thrush, and joined Anthony, giving him a look which caused him to say: 'You look like one of the Furies!'

She didn't answer him at once; she was still smarting under Doctor van Dresselhuys' amused, faintly mocking look, but as they went down the steps she asked: 'Where are we going?'

'How about that little Italian place? It's not too far to walk and it's cheap.'

He took her arm as he spoke, in much the same way, she thought resentfully, as a man might slip a collar on his dog. She freed her arm, and he muttered: 'Huh—in a bad mood, are you?' an unfair remark which hardly served to increase her good humour, so that they went down the street mentally as well as physically apart.

They patched up their differences during the evening. Anthony, with his hasty apology a little carelessly offered, plunged into a tale of how he had got the better of old Sister Tucker on Women's Medical, which, seeing that that lady was a byword in the hospital for her short temper and cursory treatment of all doctors below the rank of consultant, should have made Alexandra laugh. She did indeed smile, but it struck her that Anthony had been a bit mean with the old tartar. After all, she had been at St Job's for more than thirty years and was the best nurse the hospital had ever had; she was due to retire soon, and most people, while grumbling at her fierce tongue, secretly liked her, taking her tellings-off in good part. It was disquieting to discover that Anthony wasn't quite as nice as she had thought him to be and this feeling was heightened by the fact that she was tired and a little depressed and he had insisted on their walking back, because, as he explained, the exercise was good for them both. She wondered secretly if he grudged the price of a taxi, but later, in bed and thinking about it, she came to the conclusion that she had done him less than justice; he had his way to make, like anyone else, and probably he would end up very comfortably off because he hadn't wasted his money. She reminded herself that he was all that a girl could wish for—well, almost all, and closed her eyes. She was almost asleep when she realized that she wasn't thinking about Anthony at all but of that beastly Doctor van Dresselhuys.

She saw him the next morning. He arrived with Mr Thrush, checked the patient's progress, offered one or two suggestions in a diffident manner, and then blandly accepted her rather cold invitation to have coffee in her office. Once there, neither Mr Thrush nor he seemed disposed to leave—indeed, after ten minutes, Alexandra excused herself on the plea of work to do, and left them with the coffee pot between them, deep in a learned discussion concerning the pre-central gyrus of the brain.

She thought it highly likely that neither gentleman, although both had risen politely to their feet as she left them, had really noticed her going or heard a word of what she had said.

She had no occasion to go to her office for quite some time after that, but when she did she was surprised to find the Dutchman still there, at her desk now, writing busily. He looked up as she went in and said coolly: 'Forgive me if I don't get up—these are a few calculations and notes which must be written up immediately.'

The papers she wanted were in the desk; she edged past him and knelt down the better to reach the bottom drawer at one side of it, aware that he had stopped writing.

'Have you made it up?' he wanted to know.

She lifted her head and found his face bending over her, only a few inches away. 'I don't know what you mean,' she said indignantly.

'Don't behave like a schoolgirl,' he begged her, 'you know very well what I mean. You looked like a thunder-cloud yesterday evening, and don't try and tell me that you went dining and dancing in that elderly raincoat—besides, you walked down the street as though you hated—er—whatever his name is. You have a very eloquent back.'

'It's none of your business,' she told him hotly. 'Really…'

'Now, that is unkind; I like to see other people happy.' His voice held a mocking note. 'And you are not. I'll wager my day's fees that he walked you back.'

'It's healthy exercise,' she declared, too quickly, 'and he hasn't got a car yet—not even a Morris 1000,' she added nastily.

He ignored this piece of rudeness. 'A nice little car,' he observed smoothly, 'reliable, cheap to run and not too fast.'

She was diverted enough to exclaim: 'It doesn't look your sort of car at all,' and then remembered to add: 'Not that I am in the least interested in what you drive.'

He was staring at her. 'If I were to ask you out to dinner with me, would you come?'

'No.' The word had popped out before she had quenched the thought that she would like to, very much.

'I thought perhaps you wouldn't. Ah, well, I have survived worse disappointments. And now, young woman, if you have finished kneeling at my feet, perhaps I might continue to borrow your office for another ten minutes or so.'

She closed the drawer deliberately, clutching the papers she had sought; there was a great deal she would have liked to have said, but she thought that, on the whole, it might be better to hold her tongue, so she edged past him again and flounced out in such a bad temper that her staff nurse wanted to know if she felt ill.

She didn't see him for the rest of the day, so that by the evening she believed him gone, which was a pity because she still hadn't discovered just who he was. A good friend of Mr Thrush, that was obvious—perhaps he had a practice in England even though he was a Dutchman; that, combined with the fact that he had been at the scene of the accident, would be enough to make him take an interest in the patient.

No one had come forward to claim the girl; police inquiries, photos in the newspapers, none of these had had any results. Alexandra, hopeful of her patient's recovery, wished that she could regain consciousness, so that they could discover her name, but at the end of another two days she was still unconscious, so that Alexandra, with two days off to take, was in two minds not to take them. But common sense prevailed; she needed a break, if only to get away from Anthony, so that she could make up her mind about him. She went off duty that evening and caught the train to Dorchester by the skin of her teeth, and instead of having a quiet think as she had intended, went to sleep, only waking as the train drew in at her destination.

Jim, her younger brother, was waiting for her, still in his anorak and gumboots because he had come straight from the farm where he was finishing the last few months of his course at the Agricultural College. He greeted her with off-handed affection, caught up her case as though it had been a paper bag and led the way to where the Landrover he had borrowed was waiting.

'Nice of you to pick me up,' said Alexandra, disposing her person as comfortably as possible. 'Is Father busy?'

'Up to his eyes—'flu.' He started the engine. 'You're OK?'

'Yes, thanks. How's work?'

She sat listening to him talking about his job as he drove them at a great rate away from the town, through Cerne Abbas and then beyond, turning presently into a country road leading to the village where her father had his vast rural practice. The lights were shining a welcome as he brought the Landrover to a squealing halt before her home; a rambling, thatched house of no great size but lacking nothing of picturesque architecture.

She ran inside, glad to be home, to find her mother in the kitchen getting her supper. Mrs Dobbs was like her daughter—indeed, her husband always declared that she had been twice as pretty as her daughter when she had been younger. Even now she was still a comely woman, who hugged her daughter with real delight and advised her to go and see her father in his study while she dished up.

Doctor Dobbs was catching up on his book work, but he cast this aside as Alexandra went in, declaring that she was a sight for sore eyes, and just in time to add up his accounts for him, something she did quickly before carrying him off to the dining-room while she ate her supper.

Her parents sat at the table with her, not eating, but plying her with food and questions and answering her own questions in their turn, and presently Jim, finished for the day, joined them and then Jeff, studying to be a vet in Bristol and home for a week's leave. Only her eldest brother, Edmund, was absent; qualified a year ago, he was now a partner in his father's practice with a surgery in a neighbouring village where he lived with his wife and baby daughter.

Alexandra beamed round at them all. 'It's super to be home,' she declared. 'Every time I come, I swear I'll give up nursing.'

There was a general laugh, although Mrs Dobbs looked hopeful. She was too clever to say anything, though, but instead inquired about the girl Alexandra had been looking after. 'The local papers have had a lot to say about it,' she told her daughter, 'how strange it is that no one has come forward. And who is this doctor who saw the accident? There was a lot about him too, but no facts, if you know what I mean.'

'I don't know much about him, either,' said Alexandra. 'He—he just came in with her, you know, and when we went up to St Job's, he came too.'

'In the ambulance?'

'No—his car. A Morris 1000.'

Even her father looked up then. 'He can't be doing very well,' he observed. 'It's a nice enough car, but more suitable to elderly ladies and retired gents than to a doctor. Is he elderly?'

She shook her head. 'No—forty or thereabouts, I suppose. Perhaps younger—it's hard to tell.'

'Good-looking?' Her mother had been dying to ask that.

'Well, yes—I really didn't notice.'

It was the kind of answer to make Mrs Dobbs

dart a sharp glance at her daughter and change the subject. 'How is Anthony?' she wanted to know.

Alexandra's high forehead creased into a frown. 'Oh, all right—busy, you know.' She yawned and her mother said at once: 'You're tired, dear—bed for you. Is there anything you want to do tomorrow?'

Alexandra shook her head. 'No, Mother dear. I'll drive Father on his rounds if he'd like me to, it's a nice way of seeing the country.'

Two days of home did her a world of good; she hated going back; she always did, but there would be more days off and in the meantime work didn't seem as bad as it had done. And indeed, it wasn't; the unit had filled up, and filled up still further that morning, even though temporarily, with a case from theatre which had collapsed in the recovery room. It was late afternoon by the time the man was well enough to send back to his ward, and Alexandra was already late off duty, but before she went she paid one more visit to the girl. She was doing well now; another day and she would be sent down to the Women's Surgical ward. It was a pity that she hadn't regained consciousness, though. Alexandra bent over the quiet face and checked a breath as the girl opened her eyes.

'Hullo,' said Alexandra, and smiled reassuringly.

'Don't worry, you're in hospital. You had an accident, but you're getting better.'

The blue eyes held intelligence. 'My head aches.'

'I'm afraid it may do for a little while, but you'll be given something for it. My dear, what is your name?'

The girl looked at her for a long moment. 'I can't remember,' she spoke in a thin whisper, 'I can't remember anything.'

'Not to worry,' said Alexandra comfortably, 'it will all come back presently.' She pressed the bell beside the bed, and when a nurse came, not quite running, asked her to let the Surgical Registrar know that Mr Thrush's patient was conscious and would he come as soon as he could.

He came at once, and a few moments later, Mr Thrush with Doctor van Dresselhuys. Alexandra went to meet them and the surgeon said in tones of satisfaction: 'This is splendid, Sister, and how fortunate that Doctor van Dresselhuys should have been here with me. And now, before we see the patient, give me your observations, Sister.'

Which she did, very concisely, before going with them to the bedside.

The girl had fallen asleep with all the suddenness of a child. Alexandra counted her pulse. 'Almost normal and much stronger. How pretty she is with

all that golden hair.' She smiled at the two men.
'Like a bright penny.'

Mr Thrush nodded, but it was the Dutchman who
said quietly: 'She has no name, has she, not until
she remembers... What you just said, Sister, about
a bright penny. Could we not call her Penny
Bright?'

He too was looking down at the girl, and for no
reason at all, Alexandra suffered a pang at the expression on his face. It was ridiculous to mind; why,
they didn't even like each other, and having rescued
the girl like that must have caused him to feel
something towards her. 'It's a marvellous idea,' she
agreed at once. 'It will worry her dreadfully if we
don't call her something, and she might be like this
for some time, mightn't she?'

'One can never tell with retrograde amnesia,'
said Mr Thrush. 'A month, perhaps longer, who
knows. You'll do all in your power, I know, Sister.'
He moved to the other side of the bed. 'I think I'll
just go over her reflexes.'

Alexandra, off duty at last—for even after the
men had gone, she had to add everything to her
report—went first to the hospital entrance. Anthony
had asked her to meet him there at six o'clock, and
it was already half past that hour and she was still
in uniform. He was there all right, walking up and

down and looking impatiently at his watch every few seconds, and when she reached him and began to explain why she was late, he hardly listened, nor did he give her a chance to finish what she was saying.

'I must say,' he began furiously, 'that you have no thought for my convenience at all—here have I been waiting for the last forty minutes—the least you could have done would have been to send a message. And I can't for the life of me see why you needed to stay; the girl won't die if you leave her to someone else,' he pointed out nastily.

Alexandra sighed. She was tired and it would have been nice if she could have told him about the girl regaining consciousness and how pleased everyone was; she repressed the thought that when Anthony had been late on more than one occasion she had been expected to wait for him uncomplainingly and then listen to his weighty explanations afterwards. But he was tired too, she mustn't forget that, so she said now in a reasonable voice, 'Oh, I know that, but it helped Mr Thrush if I stayed on for a bit, because I was there when she became conscious and he wanted to know exactly what had happened. You see, she's got a retrograde amnesia—she can't remember anything, not even her name. We're going to call her Penny Bright.'

His lip curled. 'I suppose you wasted more time thinking that one up?'

She answered without thinking. 'As a matter of fact, I didn't, it was Doctor van Dresselhuys.'

'Now I know why you're late—hanging around after that Dutchman. I've seen you staring at him.'

She was cold with rage, but she kept her voice reasonably still. 'That's a silly thing to say; we don't even like each other, but you know as well as I do that you can work quite well with someone, even if you don't get on well. And I don't look at him.'

They were standing at the door, and people going in and out looked curiously at them. There was a fearful draught too and she shivered. 'Look, shall I go and change?'

She really had no wish to go out now, her evening had been spoilt and Anthony was in a vile mood, and so, she had to admit, was she.

'Don't bother,' he told her with a nasty little sneer. 'Why not go back to that fellow... I must say, Alexandra, that your behaviour is hardly what one would expect of a doctor's wife.'

That really was the last straw, the reasonableness exploded into healthy rage. 'Whose wife?' she demanded. 'I wasn't aware that I had made any plans to be a doctor's wife, and even if I had, I haven't any more,' she went on rapidly, getting a little mixed by reason of her strong feeling, 'and how dare you talk to me about my behaviour—the utter gall…' she choked on her temper, turned on her heel and crossed the hall, straight into the solid seventeen or eighteen stones of Doctor van Dresselhuys.

He caught her by the shoulders and set her back on her feet and then with his hands still there, said softly: 'Oh, dear, what a nasty habit I have of intruding into your love life!'

'It's not my love life,' she muttered in a fine rage. 'I haven't got one, and I wish you wouldn't keep…' She stopped and sniffed, aware that at any moment she was going to burst into tears. 'If you would let go of me,' she besought him, and when he did, tore off through the hospital until she reached the haven of her room. A hearty burst of tears relieved her feelings enormously, and thankful that there was no one else off duty, she went along to make a pot of tea and then, very much refreshed, had a bath. By the time her friends came off duty after supper, she looked very much as usual and was able to join in their talk as though she hadn't a care in the world. It was only after all the various doors had closed and it was quiet and dark that she got out her writing case and found a pen.

Miss Trott showed considerable astonishment when Alexandra, her written resignation in her hand, presented herself in the office the following morning. She heard her rather feeble reasons for leaving without comment and only when she had finished did she remark: 'This is a great surprise to me, Sister Dobbs, I had come to regard you as one of my more permanent senior nurses. Naturally, I had expected that you might leave in order to get married...' She paused expectantly, but Alexandra had nothing to say to that, and she frowned slightly, thwarted out of the speech she had intended to make so that Alexandra might be persuaded to change her mind. She sighed. 'Who is to take your place?'

'Well, Staff Nurse Thorne is very good, Miss Trott, she's been my right hand for more than two years, she would be perfectly capable of taking over the unit, and everyone likes her.'

'You are determined to leave, Sister Dobbs?'

'Yes, quite determined, Miss Trott.'

'And not, I fancy, entirely for the reasons which you have given me?'

'No, Miss Trott.'

'Well, in that case I must accept your resignation, although with the greatest reluctance. And I will consider Staff Nurse Thorne for the post.' She smiled faintly in dismissal. Alexandra was one of her favourites, although she was careful not to show partiality for any one of her staff. That she was labouring under strong feelings was obvious to Miss Trott's experienced eye, trained to notice such things. Equally obvious was the fact that she was to be told nothing but a string of flimsy reasons as to why she wished to leave. She sighed and pulled a sheaf of papers towards her, aware of a number of half buried, wistful thoughts.

Alexandra's thoughts were neither wistful nor half buried; they were angry and a little frightened; she had burnt her boats behind her for the silliest of reasons and on an impulse. She had surely made it clear to Anthony that she didn't wish to marry him; they could have continued to be friends and he would have found another girl, more amenable than she so that she could have stayed on in the unit and everything would have been settled in a nice, civilized fashion, but upon reflection, it wouldn't have done at all. Anthony wasn't the kind of man to accept her as a friend once all idea of marriage between them had been scotched and meeting him each day would have been embarrassing to them both. Not only that, she reminded herself, he had been unreasonably ill-tempered, shouting at her and making snide remarks about Doctor van Dresselhuys. Not that she had any sympathy with that gentleman, always poking his large arrogant nose into her affairs.

With difficulty she brought her mind back to her own problems; she had a month in which to find another job—time enough, indeed, a few weeks at home while she looked around might be a good thing—just what she needed to cure the vague restlessness she had felt for the last few days.

She quickened her footsteps, back to the ICU, confident that she had her future well in hand.

CHAPTER THREE

IT was the second week of November, which meant that Alexandra would be free to leave well before Christmas, a sound reason to postpone the finding of a job until after the festive season. And indeed, during the ensuing weeks, she found herself singularly loath to set about serious job-hunting; she had made several tentative inquiries and met with encouraging replies, but she found herself unable to make up her mind about any of them, something which puzzled her just as much as it puzzled her family and friends. In the end she concluded that it was because she didn't want to leave Penny Bright; the girl was making excellent progress now, down in Women's Surgical, and each day she became prettier, only her memory, for the moment at least, had gone, and without relations or friends to stimulate it, it was proving a difficult task to break down the barrier her accident had caused. Mr Thrush was of the opinion that it would return, given time and patience, in the meantime he was satisfied with her progress. Alexandra went to visit her each day, usually as she was going off duty in the early evening, and it was on one of these occasions, two weeks or more after she had decided to leave, that Penny surprised her by saying: 'Doctor van Dresselhuys says that I am almost well. I shall be glad to leave here, though everyone has been very nice to me.'

Alexandra smiled. 'Well, of course, why shouldn't they be?' and could not prevent herself from asking: 'Does he come often, the doctor?'

Penny answered readily. 'Oh, yes, every week. He brings me books and magazines now that I may read a little and he shows me pictures of places and asks me if I know them. Sometimes he's stern, though, and says I must do as I'm told...'

'Why does he say that?'

'Well, sometimes I don't do as Sister tells me and then I get giddy—I shan't be giddy for always, shall I?'

'No, of course not, Penny, but you gave your head a nasty bang, you know, and it'll take a little time to get quite well.'

She gave the girl sitting so docilely in the chair a motherly look. What a charming creature she was; no wonder the housemen made a beeline for her the moment they came into the ward, and so, apparently, did Doctor van Dresselhuys. She frowned, annoyed at having thought about him at all; she had dismissed him to the back of her mind days ago—

she had tried to dismiss him altogether, but he had refused to go—and now, with just one remark from Penny, here he was again, every line of his handsome, aloof face well remembered, every note of his deep voice ringing in her ears.

She found herself wondering if she would encounter him on one of his visits, but either he had just gone or was expected shortly; he was never there when she was. After a few days she came to the conclusion that he didn't want to meet her again.

She was finding the month hard to get through; she and Anthony couldn't avoid meeting each other, and although she kept up a semblance of friendliness towards him, he chose to ignore this, behaving as though his feelings were much injured, and taking care to let everyone see it. She found herself longing to be gone even though her plans for the future were still vague. Even the news that Penny was considered well enough to leave hospital, while delighting her, did nothing to spur her on to the tiresome task of finding another job, let alone make up her mind where she wanted to go.

A decision which, as it turned out, she didn't have to make, for the very next day, a few minutes after she had gained her room after her day's duty, the floor telephone shrilled, bidding her go all the way downstairs again because Doctor van Dresselhuys would like a word with her.

Not in the best of tempers at this infringement of her free time, she dug her feet back into her shoes, put back the cap she had just taken off her rather untidy head, and trailed down four flights of stairs, to find him pacing impatiently to and fro in the hall.

The moment he saw her, however, he stopped his perambulations and came towards her, reaching the bottom step at the same time as she did, so that she found her eyes almost on a level with his. They stared at each other silently until she asked in a nettled tone: 'You wanted to see me, Doctor van Dresselhuys?'

'Yes. Penny is leaving the hospital in two days' time, of course you know that.' His voice was almost curt. 'I understand that you are also leaving and have no immediate plans for the future. Penny has nowhere to go and until such time as she regains her memory, or her family come forward to claim her, my aunt has offered to give her a home. It is, of course, out of the question that she should do this without help. It would oblige me—us, if you would accompany her as a companion—nurse, whatever you like to call yourself, until her future is assured—at a not too distant date, I hope. We would naturally pay you your present salary.'

Alexandra opened her mouth and closed it again. She had been very much surprised at his offer, and now she was still more surprised to find that her instinctive response had been to say yes without even bothering to think it over. But she was a level-headed girl, not liking to be rushed into anything, so she thought about it for a few minutes, then: 'That would be a great deal too much money,' she observed. 'Looking after one girl is hardly the same as running a big unit.'

He disregarded this. 'You'll come?' His cool assumption that she would come piqued her. 'I was going home for Christmas…'

'Would you have gone if you had remained at St Job's?'

Honesty compelled her to say that she wouldn't, even though it annoyed her very much to have to confess it. He nodded in a satisfied way, which annoyed her even more. 'Then I can take it as settled?'

'No, you can't,' she snapped. 'Do you always bulldoze your own way over other people? You've told me nothing; merely asked me to take a job. I don't even know where your aunt lives.'

He smiled at her with a sudden charm which took her breath.

'I've annoyed you, I'm sorry. I've been careless

of your feelings and quite thoughtless; that is because I have been considering this plan for the last few days and I very much want you to take the job. You see, Penny is fond of you, and you have helped her a good deal even though she hasn't been in your care for the last couple of weeks. You are a sensible woman and resourceful too, and I think—so does Mr Thrush—that if anyone can help Penny to overcome her amnesia, you are that one. Besides, Aunt Euphemia likes you.'

He paused and turned away to stare out of the small window, although there was nothing to see in the outside dark. 'And you are quite right, I have told you nothing. My aunt has a small house—a cottage—in Suffolk. Rather remote, I should warn you, the nearest town of any size is Needham Market, and that's no size at all. The cottage is a mile from the nearest village, Denningham. Do you drive?'

'Yes.'

'Ah, well, there will be no problem there, and little or nothing for you to do other than keep Penny under your eye, look to her health and try constantly, without her being too aware of it, to coax back her memory, even her name would help. We have decided to wait another two or three weeks, and if there are no developments during that time, then we shall have to do some more thinking. It is extraordinary that none of her family or friends have come forward; she may of course be in the unhappy position of having neither, but I hardly think that is the case.' He gave her a direct look. 'Would you mind very much about Christmas?'

It surprised her then, that although she was devoted to her family and had been looking forward to seeing them, she didn't mind so very much. 'Well...' she began, and he interrupted her with: 'Could we compromise? You are due to leave in two days' time, aren't you? The same time as Penny. Could you not go home for a few days and then return here to collect her and take her down to my aunt's house? I'm sure that I could persuade Mr Thrush to keep Penny another few days if necessary.'

'Well,' said Alexandra again, 'yes, all right, Doctor. It's true that I haven't decided on another job yet; I've been offered several and I don't really care for any of them.' She added in a burst of honesty, 'Only there's just one condition, I won't come unless you agree to pay me less money.'

'Why?' He looked faintly amused, so that she went on awkwardly: 'Well, it—it will cost you a lot of money to have Penny, even for three weeks, and then me on top of that...'

'Now that is extremely thoughtful of you, Miss Dobbs.' His eyes flickered down to his well-worn suit and then back to hers, and although his face was blandly friendly, she could have sworn that he was laughing silently, so that she pinkened. 'I accept your condition, dear girl, and thank you. It is quite true that there will be some expense in the matter of clothes and so on for Penny; you will be of the greatest help there, for Aunty is a thought old-fashioned, and I—I know very little about such matters.'

His voice was as bland as his face and she frowned a little uneasily, but he gave her no time to ponder his words. 'I won't keep you any longer,' he told her decisively, 'I'm sure that you have plans for your evening.' His manner became almost friendly. 'I hope I shall not be the cause of annoying young—er—Ferris again, keeping you talking like this.'

There was the faintest query in his voice; he would know about her and Anthony—everyone in the hospital knew by now, and there was no use in pretending they didn't. 'You don't have to be polite about it,' she said, 'Anthony and I...well, we agreed that we didn't suit each other.' She caught the doctor's eyes bent upon her and saw their sardonic gleam.

'We had a flaming row,' she amended, 'that's really why I'm leaving.'

He answered her in a matter-of-fact voice. 'You were entirely unsuited, even to someone as disinterested as myself, that was obvious.'

Her fine eyes flashed. 'Oh, was it indeed? And what business is it of yours, might I ask?'

'None at all—I have just told you that I am quite disinterested—I merely made an observation.'

She took instant exception to this. 'Well, don't, I'm not a child to be told what to do.'

He studied her rather heated countenance. 'How old are you, Sister Dobbs?'

She wasn't a girl to be coy about such things. 'Twenty-seven,' she told him with the faintest lift of her eyebrows, and he said instantly, half laughing: 'And I am thirty-six—that is what you wished to know, was it not?' He smiled and held out his hand. 'A pleasant stay at your home, and my thanks for taking the job. And now I must be going.'

She felt her hand wrung gently and remembered to ask: 'Will I have instructions when I get back here?'

'Yes, all arrangements will have been made for you.' He sounded suddenly impatient to be gone. 'Good-bye, Miss Dobbs.' He nodded briefly and walked to the door where he turned to say: 'I think

I shall call you Alexandra—Miss Dobbs doesn't suit you in the least.'

She stood where he had left her, looking at the door long after he had closed it, trying to make up her mind if the feeling making itself felt inside her was dislike for him, or whether she liked him very much. A bit of both, she concluded sensibly, and went back to her room to fetch some money so that she might telephone home.

Her mother, as was usual, was a little incoherent, for she had a habit of speaking her thoughts aloud in the middle of a perfectly rational conversation, casting her listeners, unless they knew her well, into confusion. But Alexandra was used to her; through the tangle of regret at her not being home for Christmas, delight at her impending visit, the complete breakdown of the village organ and Mrs Watt's total inability to speak her lines right in the nativity play being got up by the WI, Alexandra deduced that her parent was resigned to her taking a new job at such an awkward time, and when that lady asked suddenly if she and Anthony had quarrelled irrevocably, Alexandra was able to assure her quite cheerfully that yes, they had, to which her mother replied: 'Oh, well—there's that nice Dutch doctor.'

'Mother dear,' said Alexandra, very clearly, 'we

don't even like each other particularly. Besides, he's years older than me.'

'How old?' demanded her mother.

'Thirty-six.'

'Just right,' replied Mrs Dobbs happily. 'You just wait and see…'

'Mother,' Alexandra was laughing now, 'you're incorrigible! I must go, see you in two days' time—ask Father to meet me if he can, will you?'

She went back upstairs, and because she had nothing better to do, began on the interesting task of sorting out what clothes she would need. No uniform, the doctor had said, and since Aunty lived in such a retired manner, presumably no evening clothes. She decided on serviceable tweeds and sweaters and a rather nice trouser suit she had only just bought. Her winter coat was tweed too, russet and brown—and there was a knitted cap and scarf to go with it as well as a fine wool dress to wear beneath it—with those she should be able to get through a couple of weeks in the depths of the country; as an afterthought she added a silk jersey dress in a dark burgundy red and some elegant shoes—after all, she would be there for Christmas and Miss Thrums, however isolated, must surely have a few friends to drop in. Lastly, as a concession to the probable wet weather, she added an elderly anorak, hooded, shabby, but still useful.

Two days later she went home, to be met by her father in Dorchester. A quiet man, who said little but saw a great deal, he touched lightly upon her new job, expressed regret that her visit was to be such a short one, and volunteered his opinion that Suffolk was a charming part of England, even in midwinter. She agreed absently and then asked: 'Father, does it seem strange to you that no one has come forward to claim Penny?'

'Not really. It's a sad fact that a great many young people today leave home and find work in another part of the country—she's young, this Penny of yours? But old enough to work for her living, presumably—and she could drive a car. A car, I'm told, stolen from a garage in the Midlands. Not that she need necessarily have taken it—someone she knew might have done that and lent it to her, without her being aware of the circumstances. In that case whoever that was isn't likely to come forward, is he—or she? They would be accused of theft.'

'I hadn't thought of that. But her parents...'

'Dead—on holiday abroad, there are a dozen possibilities. In any case, dear, I shouldn't worry your head about it—the thing is to help her to regain her memory; once that is done, those looking after her can sort things out. Mr Thrush, isn't it, and this Dutch doctor—a friend of his, you say?'

Alexandra was looking at the familiar landscape. 'Yes—and quite a close one, I imagine, though I don't think he's anything very special. He's—well, he's a bit shabby, I suppose, though his clothes are very good and he doesn't seem to have a car—the Morris is his aunt's. I think he must be a GP in Holland, though I haven't asked.'

Her father gave her a quick look. 'No reason why you should, is there? I daresay Mr Thrush and he knew each other when they were younger men.'

'He's not that old,' said Alexandra sharply, and then, happy to change the conversation: 'Oh, look, there's old Mrs Duke.' She waved as they passed and added happily, 'It's lovely to be home again, Father.'

The two days went in a flash; she had no sooner arrived than she found herself packing her case again, wishing with all her heart that she had refused to take on a job so soon after leaving St Job's. Only a fool, she thought crossly, would have allowed herself to be persuaded to miss Christmas at home—she didn't even need the money; she had a little saved and her father, while not overblessed with the world's goods, would have raised no ob-

jection to her staying home for a few weeks, or for
that matter, for as long as she had wanted to. But
some of her dissatisfaction disappeared when she
reached the hospital and found Penny eagerly waiting for her. The girl seemed delighted to see her
again, tucking a hand into Alexandra's arm and
looking confidingly into her face. 'I was terrified
that you wouldn't come,' she told her.

Alexandra thought how young and helpless she
looked. 'Well, I did, didn't I?' she reassured her,
'so now you don't need to worry any more.'

They went by train to Needham Market, a tiresome journey, but as Mr Thrush had pointed out, a
good opportunity to note how Penny reacted to her
surroundings. But she didn't, she sat looking out of
the window, not really noticing anything, and by
the time they arrived she was getting tired. It was
a relief to find Miss Thrums on the platform, who,
after a brisk greeting, ushered them out of the station to where the Morris 1000 was standing. It was
six or seven miles to Denningham, and apparently
Miss Thrums knew every inch of the way blind-
folded; nothing else could have accounted for the
speed at which she drove. Alexandra, sitting beside
her with Penny tucked up on the back seat, was
thankful that the rolling, open countryside afforded
a good view for some distance ahead of them, so

that any oncoming traffic had time to take evasive action before Miss Thrums ran them down. 'You drive, I hear,' she remarked. 'Taro was pleased about that—he has the oddest notion that I'm not a good driver.'

'Taro?' asked Alexandra. Such a strange name, but it suited him.

'Yes, dear—my nephew, after his father, you know. His mother was my sister—such a dear girl and younger than I. She died two years ago. His father is still alive although retired, and he has three sisters. He and I have always been great friends.' She took her eye off the road to give Alexandra a searching glance. 'Such a dear boy.'

'Yes? Well, I expect he is,' said Alexandra awkwardly, and was glad when her companion changed the subject.

The doctor had been right; Denningham was very small, a handful of lovely old cottages, a village shop and church and the manor house standing behind the stark lines of the winter trees. They drove through it, still much too fast, and presently turned off the road into a narrow lane running through ploughed fields and, presently, a copse. The cottage had buried itself halfway through the little cluster of trees and undergrowth, a Hans Andersen masterpiece, small and gabled and narrow-windowed, each gable carved with a variety of animals' heads, its front door a ponderous affair which one would have to stoop to enter.

'My little place,' Miss Thrums pointed out happily, and shot the car with abandon up the short, muddy drive to the door and leapt out with all the agility of a fourteen-year-old. 'You bring in Penny,' she advised Alexandra, 'we can fetch the bags later.'

Penny, clinging to Alexandra's arm, looked around her with interest before saying in a disappointed voice: 'It's so quiet—aren't there any houses close by?'

'None at all,' stated her hostess cheerfully, 'but you'll find so much to do that I doubt if you will notice that—and you've got Alexandra and me for company.' She glanced at Alexandra. 'Bed?' she asked.

'I think so—if I might take her supper up, she's very tired.'

They mounted the narrow staircase, a spiral fitted into the tiny hall, and Miss Thrums opened a door on the landing. The room was small but very pretty and Alexandra noticed with approval that it contained all the comforts which a young girl might look for: magazines, a handful of books, a tin of biscuits, a warm dressing gown on the bed and matching slippers. Miss Thrums must have gone to a good deal of trouble and expense.

Because Penny had nothing to say, she said warmly: 'What a lovely room! Look, Penny, everything you could possibly want,' and when the girl didn't respond: 'You're tired; I'm going to help you to bed. You'll feel marvellous in the morning.'

It was an hour later when she went downstairs to join Miss Thrums. Penny had eaten her supper like an obedient child and had been tucked up for the night, and she had unpacked her own things in the room next to Penny's; a room as pretty as her patient's. The little house was charming and its sitting room was surprisingly large, with glass doors taking the place of one wall, so that wherever one sat, there was a view. It was dark now, of course, but the thin, chilly moon made it possible to see beyond a stretch of grass to the trees which hedged it. Alexandra, sipping sherry opposite her hostess, saw something move out there in the dark, and although she said nothing, Miss Thrums, who was watching her, said happily: 'The deer come each evening—I leave food out for them and sometimes they come right up to the doors. There are badgers too.' She put down her glass. 'Come and have supper, my dear, and tell me exactly what is to be done for that poor girl upstairs.'

They settled easily and quickly into a pleasant routine; breakfast in bed for Penny, the preparing of which Alexandra had persuaded Miss Thrums was one of her nursing duties, and when she had been settled comfortably against her pillows, breakfast for the two of them in the cheerful little kitchen. Miss Thrums, in a sensible tweed skirt and a twin set, her nice face free of make-up, her hair scraped back into its firm bun, made the coffee and toast while Alexandra, in slacks and a thick sweater, her hair tied back, laid a table under the window, where they had their simple meal and a pleasant gossip before washing up together.

Alexandra went up to Penny then, making beds and tidying up and keeping an eye on her while she dressed, and after the first few days, she began to discover things about her patient; Penny liked pretty things—and certainly Miss Thrums had provided her with a charming wardrobe even though it was scanty—but only if the pretty things were hers; she thought nothing of the dainty china and small silver ornaments Miss Thrums dusted so lovingly each day, she thought nothing of the polished Regency table and chairs either, nor did she show any interest in the small collection of quite valuable oil paintings in the sitting room; she didn't like Jock, the elderly Golden Labrador, who was Miss

Thrums' constant companion, and it wasn't just dogs; she had flung Sambo the kitten off her lap with a rough pettishness which amounted to dislike. This could very well be the result of her accident, Alexandra conceded, so she did her best to keep the animals away from her patient and struggled to cope with Penny's increasing peevishness.

It had seemed nothing of a job when she had accepted it, but within the first few days she had discovered that it wasn't going to be all roses; Penny was irritable if she didn't get her own way, and was prone to sulk; Alexandra ignored this as far as possible and pegged away at trying to find some clue as to the girl's past. But in this she was unlucky, for there was no response to her carefully put questions, only blank looks or a total disinterest; it was almost as though Penny didn't want to remember, she thought uneasily. But slowly she was building up some sort of picture of the girl, although whether it was a true one she was unable to decide. The pretty manners and the charming air of helplessness were there, but she made no secret of the fact that she was bored with country life; she found nothing to do in the dear little house, its treasures held no pleasure for her, the garden she ignored, and although she was happy enough sitting by the fire with a magazine, she made no attempt to start a conversation with her companions, although she answered readily enough when they addressed her.

Was this bored, rather silent girl the real Penny? Alexandra wondered, or the result of the accident—she had certainly been a different girl in the hospital, and could it be that she had been accustomed to a busy town life with plenty of people around her? She took her to Needham Market with the car one morning and tried to find out, and was pleased with the mild success of the outing. Penny had enjoyed the shops and had commented at some length over the clothes, and once or twice Alexandra had been puzzled of the way she spoke, as though she was choosing her words carefully, concealing something. But when she asked: 'Do you feel you're almost remembering something, Penny?' she was met with a blank look and a quick: 'No, no—oh, if only I could!'

But back at the cottage again, she lapsed once more into boredom and Alexandra consoled herself by remembering that it was early days yet, patience was needed as well as firmness and kindness. Miss Thrums agreed with her, doing her share by cooking nourishing meals of an astonishing variety, giving it her opinion that good food was absolutely essential to any young creature who had been ill.

Alexandra came upon her one morning, counting the money in her old-fashioned purse, and wondered if housing and feeding Penny and herself was proving too great a strain on her resources, but it was impossible to ask; Miss Thrums wasn't that kind of person.

At least by the end of the week, Penny had improved physically; she had a pretty colour now and she had gained some weight, her charming face when she was pleased about something was full of vivacity and her hair, after a good deal of experimenting, was now arranged to cover the scar of her operation, but there was no denying the fact that for most of the time she was listless. If only, thought Alexandra, vainly trying to interest her in a game of cards, she would show some animation.

She was to have her wish; Doctor van Dresselhuys arrived on Saturday afternoon, walking up to the front door with a rather battered travelling bag swinging from one hand. She saw him first, but before she could say anything, Penny had looked up and seen him too. She was out of her chair and through the front door like a flash, to fling herself into the doctor's arms, her face alight, her voice so gay and happy that Alexandra could hardly believe that this was the quiet, morose girl she had been struggling to cheer up during the last week. Perhaps, she thought worriedly, this had been the reason for the girl's changed behaviour; she had been unhappy without the doctor.

CHAPTER FOUR

HE had come, he informed his aunt as he kissed her cheek, for the week-end so that he could check on Penny—he tweaked the golden hair as he spoke and smiled down at her, clinging still to his arm. It was almost as an afterthought that he turned to Alexandra to greet her briskly, uttering a few conventional phrases which required nothing more than a smile and a murmur in reply. It was Penny who took almost all his attention for the rest of the day, and quite rightly so, Alexandra reminded herself, genuinely glad to see the girl so changed; she was the life and soul of the party, laughing delightedly at anything the doctor said, telling him, not always quite truthfully, of the things she had done during the week, touching upon Alexandra's guardianship in a joking voice which almost but not quite made her out to be a bossy autocrat. Everyone laughed at that, though Alexandra stifled a puzzled disquiet; Penny wasn't meaning to be unkind, she was thoughtless, that was all.

She ignored the doctor's thoughtful stare and went, at Miss Thrums' request, to feed Rover, she

71

took him for a walk too, not bothering to go back to the little group by the sitting room fire. Instead, she plodded along the lanes, taking the poor dog for a much longer run than his middle age called for, and feeling unaccountably put out.

They were still sitting where she had left them, talking about Christmas, and from the look on Penny's face she had no trouble at all in guessing that the doctor was going to spend it with them. 'I'll be over on Christmas Eve,' he promised them, 'though heaven knows at what time.'

'But you'll come again—before then?' It was Penny who asked, and the adoring expression on her face would have flattered a block of granite.

'Good lord, Penny—Christmas is only just round the corner and I'm a working man. I'll just about have enough time to buy the presents. What do you want?' He smiled at her laughingly and she said at once:

'A dress—Oh, Taro, a blue dress, I'll show you…' She searched the pile of magazines she had been reading when he arrived and handed him a *Vogue*, still searching for the right page. It was a beautiful dress—pale blue wool with ruffles round its neck and wrists—it was also wildly expensive. He studied it carefully and said at length: 'Well, we'll see what we can do,' then cast the magazine aside and looked at Miss Thrums. 'And you, Aunty?'

'Well, dear boy, if it's not too expensive a present, I do very much want a new wheelbarrow.'

There was a ripple of laughter from them all as he turned to Alexandra. 'And you, my dear Miss Dobbs?'

He had spoken her name as though it had amused him, and there was no earthly reason why he couldn't have called her Alexandra like everyone else—it merely served to set her apart. She swallowed a sad resentment and plunged gaily: 'Oh, I'll settle for sapphires; necklace, earrings, bracelet, ring—the lot... Oh, and a little gold revolving angel playing Christmas tunes.'

She managed a smile as gay as her voice had been. 'Isn't it fun asking for impossible things? And now tell us what you would like, Doctor.'

He became all at once bland. 'Since you ask—a very small house in the country, just like this one, adequately furnished and suitably occupied, of course.'

His aunt smiled faintly and said nothing. Alexandra longed to put the question Penny instantly asked. 'Who? Who would be there?'

His face was as bland as his voice had been. 'Why, a wife, naturally enough, and since it would be Christmas, as many children as could be fitted in comfortably.'

Penny gave a little trill of laughter. 'Don't be so stuffy, Taro,' she begged him. 'People don't get married these days—we're free to do just what we like.' She pouted prettily at him. 'Wouldn't I do instead?'

'Don't beg questions,' he told her, 'and kindly remember that I'm old enough to be stuffy if I want to be,' and Alexandra saw his suddenly alert eyes; perhaps he had thought as she had done. Penny had expressed her modern ideas quite spontaneously; perhaps a subconscious memory from the past; a tiny clue, not even that, but worth remembering.

He changed the conversation at once and presently Alexandra went to get the supper, telling Miss Thrums that she had nothing better to do, a rather unfortunate remark which caused the doctor to stare at her as she went out of the room.

Sunday passed without her seeing much of him; he went to church with his aunt in the morning, and after lunch he took Penny for a walk, suggesting that she might like a few hours to herself. She occupied them in sitting at the little walnut writing desk in the sitting room, composing a falsely bright letter to her mother, and then busied herself getting the tea so that Miss Thrums might have a little time with her nephew. He was to leave early the next morning, he had mentioned casually, and had gone on to ask her one or two routine questions about Penny in much the same manner as he would have done on a hospital ward. She answered him with professional brevity and went up to bed at the end of a totally unsatisfactory evening feeling so low-spirited that she began to wonder if she was sickening for something.

She wakened early, surprised to find that it was already light. The thought that it wasn't raining got her out of bed, to dress quickly and steal downstairs, take her coat from the old-fashioned hat stand in the tiny hall, and let herself out into the garden.

It was a jewel of a morning—a few hours of autumn allowed to slip between the dark winter days, bringing with it a faded blue sky and the very first rays of the sun, sending the light mist into lacy spirals and giving the dewdrops on the cobwebs a diamond sparkle. She walked across the grass to the further end, where the garden petered out in a charming tangle of small trees and shrubs. There were birds there, twittering softly, and she took the slice of bread she had purloined from the kitchen and began to scatter crumbs.

She didn't hear the doctor's silent approach

across the short grass. His quiet: 'Good morning, Alexandra,' caused her to jump and the little party of blackbirds, thrushes and sparrows which had collected around her took instant shelter in the trees. She wished him good morning with faint reproach and he grinned as he took the last of the bread from her and began to scatter it, whistling a variety of bird calls as he did so.

'Show-off,' said Alexandra crossly, and he grinned again, like a schoolboy.

'One of my very few talents,' he explained with mock humility. 'Look, here they all are, back again.'

They stood quietly while the birds finished their crumbs and then flew away. 'A lovely morning,' observed the doctor.

'Heavenly—the mist makes everything look like fairyland...'

'A cobweb morning—that's what it's called in these parts—did you not know that?'

She smiled up at him. 'No, I didn't. It's a beautiful description.'

He said seriously: 'Yes, and you are a beautiful girl, Alexandra.' He bent his head to kiss her, taking his time about it, then: 'I have to go now,' he told her abruptly, and went.

She heard no sounds of a car; presumably he

would walk to the village and pick up the local taxi. Of course he would have a car in Holland; he would need one for his work, though it would be an expensive business to bring it over each time he came. Probably he had spent several years saving to buy a practice and now he would have to live economically until he had got firmly established. She remembered how he had wished for a little house and a wife and children, but unless the girl he married was prepared to live on a budget for several years, he would have to wait for his wish. The idea saddened her; she discovered to her surprise that she didn't dislike him any more, rather she found herself wishing with all her heart that he might get his own way, but he was kind too—she had seen that with his treatment of Penny—the thought brought her up short; perhaps she was the wife he wanted. Perhaps that was why he had arranged for her to stay with his aunt, knowing that she would be safe until she had recovered sufficiently for her to marry him—and she adored him too. Alexandra had up till now thought of her flagrant worship of him as a child's gratitude for what he had done for her, now she wasn't so sure. She was very young, of course, but what had age got to do with loving someone?

She wished suddenly that she knew him better;

looking back, he had seemed more approachable at the hospital—that time in her office, for instance...she shivered, the beauty of the morning was fading already. It had been an illusion of autumn, quickly past. She went indoors, feeling sad.

Penny was difficult all the next day; the doctor had gone without wishing her good-bye and she had sulked and grumbled for hours after he had gone; gone to bed early with a headache, and got up the next morning in one of her most difficult moods. In the end Alexandra was forced to take her for a long walk so that Miss Thrums might have some peace. By bedtime she had contrived to get Penny into a more cheerful frame of mind, but it had been exhausting work; she went to bed herself feeling quite worn out.

The preparations for Christmas kept them all occupied. Luckily Miss Thrums, despite her sensible appearance, was strongly addicted to old habits and customs. Holly was searched for and hung, mistletoe was hung too. Alexandra made a note of the places so that when the doctor came, she could avoid them, not admitting to herself that she was a little afraid that he might kiss her again and that she would like it too much. She had enjoyed the kiss in the garden, but it mustn't become a habit... She engaged herself in making paper chains, while

Penny sat beside her, enrapt in *Harper's Bazaar* and *Vogue*. Christmas, despite all their efforts, didn't seem to mean much to her, nor did the simple service in the village church. She only seemed to be interested in pretty clothes and the doctor, and Alexandra, being a wise young woman, allowed her to have her head; she took her shopping as often as was practical and lent a sympathetic ear to all that Penny had to say about him. He was always Taro, never the doctor; she spoke of him as though she had known him for years and with a possessiveness which set Alexandra's teeth on edge. But it opened the way for carefully put questions from time to time, in the hope of ringing the bell of Penny's lost memory.

She had no luck, though, only it seemed to her that the girl's character was emerging, bit by bit; modern—very modern, with a strange feckless attitude towards life which shocked Alexandra. She cared for nothing which wasn't connected with her own comfort, and although she disguised her self-ishness under a compelling charm, it was selfish-ness, all the same. Alexandra wondered if her accident could have changed her to that extent—there had been no indication of that, but head injuries were unpredictable at times.

They shopped for Christmas presents, of course,

Alexandra found a soft mohair stole for Miss
Thrums and a silk scarf for Penny in the soft blue
which she liked so much. It would go very well
with the grey tweed coat Miss Thrums had given
her when she left the hospital. And as for the doctor, she came across a small leather-bound pocket-
book which seemed very suitable as a gift. Penny
shopped too, and when Alexandra asked where she
had got the money from, careful to ask it casually
for fear that Penny should feel that she was prying,
she was told that Taro had given it to her so that
she might buy presents for anyone she wanted to
give them to. There was a faint whine in her voice
as she said it and a hint of reproach that no one
else had thought of doing the same. But on the
whole the days were happy ones, and once the little
house was decorated to the standard Miss Thrums
had set, Alexandra turned her attention to the
kitchen. Miss Thrums would see to the turkey and
the Christmas pudding and all the other festive food
she had been buying, but there was still plenty to
be done—potatoes to peel and sprouts to clean and
almonds to blanch and raisins to stone; Miss
Thrums, being old-fashioned, didn't believe in the
new-fangled plastic packs. Half the fun, she pointed
out, was in the preparation, and Alexandra, whose
mother shared her hostess's views, agreed.

It was cold on Christmas Eve; the doctor hadn't sent word as to when he was to arrive, they weren't even sure how he intended to come. 'Sometimes he flies,' said his aunt vaguely, 'sometimes he comes by boat—he might not get here until Christmas morning.'

It seemed as though her words might prove right; there was no sign of him by tea-time and even though they held supper back as long as they could, he still hadn't arrived. At eleven o'clock Alexandra persuaded Penny, not without difficulty, to go to bed. 'Even if he comes now, he'll be tired,' she pointed out reasonably. 'All he'll want is a warm drink and his bed.' So Penny went to bed and Alexandra, going upstairs half an hour later, found her soundly asleep.

It was almost twelve o'clock when Miss Thrums allowed her straight back to sag a little. 'My dear,' she said, 'I feel a little tired, would you mind very much staying up just a little longer—just in case Taro should come? There's soup warming on the Aga, and you know where the whisky is.'

Alexandra was playing with Sambo, curled up on her lap. 'No, of course I don't mind, Miss Thrums, though I don't expect he'll come until the morning now. How long shall I stay up?'

Miss Thrums looked vague. She had, come to

think of it, thought Alexandra, looked vague about her nephew's arrival all day. 'Oh, another hour, my dear. You're sure you don't mind?'

She went to let Rover out into the garden while she wound the clock just as she did every night, and then with him for company, trod quietly up the stairs. The little house was very quiet after she had gone.

Alexandra made no effort to move because of disturbing Sambo; she sat doing nothing in the softly lighted room, watching the dim outlines of the trees against the moonlit sky. The curtains were never pulled; she could see clearly into the garden—the deer were there as they usually were and it was all very peaceful. So peaceful that she dozed off, to waken as the clock struck midnight. Christmas Day, and she should really go to bed. She lifted the kitten gently on to the old shawl he liked for his bed and went to the window to look out. The doctor was outside, sitting hunched up in a sheepskin jacket, his bag at his feet, packages piled neatly beside him. He smiled at her through the glass and when she made haste to open the window, wished her a happy Christmas in a voice which held no impatience.

Alexandra urged him inside, snatched up the nearest of the parcels and closed the window on the icy air outside. 'You must be frozen!' she exclaimed. 'However long have you been there? Why didn't you tap on the glass?' She had him by the sleeve and was pushing him towards the fire. 'You'll catch your death,' she added gloomily.

'I'm not frozen,' he assured her cheerfully, and glanced at the clock. 'I got here at five minutes to midnight, and you looked so comfortable sitting there snoring. I hadn't the heart to wake you.'

'Snoring? I wasn't—I don't...how could you have heard through the window?'

He chuckled. 'You rattled the glass,' he assured her. 'Where's the whisky?'

She fetched it. 'There's some soup. I'll get it.' She slipped past him and he put out a hand and caught her arm. 'Nice of you to stay up,' he said.

'Well, I didn't—at least, your aunt was tired and she asked me...and Penny wanted to keep awake, really she did, only she's not quite well yet.'

He let go her arm. 'Dear Miss Dobbs, so quick with the practical answer.' And when she looked at him she saw the smiling mockery on his face; she saw the tiredness there too. 'You're tired,' she said gently. 'Drink your whisky and I'll get that soup. How did you get here?'

'Upon the wings of the wind.' He smiled unexpectedly and she smiled back as she went to the kitchen.

She brought a tray; soup somehow didn't seem enough for such a large man. She loaded it with bread and cheese and mince pies, and set the coffee on the heat before she carried these back into the sitting room. He was stretched out in a chair, his eyes closed, although he opened them as she put the tray down. 'Food,' he observed happily, and fell to.

'It's useful to be practical sometimes,' said Alexandra dryly as she served the soup.

She fetched the coffee presently and poured herself a mug as well, sitting on the leather camel stool close to the fire to drink it. She had had to edge her way in rather, for the doctor's long legs took up a great deal of room. They spoke hardly at all until he had polished off the last of the mince pies and drained the coffee jug; he certainly had a mammoth appetite, but then there was a great deal of him. He didn't look tired any more, indeed, he sat up and dragged the pile of parcels towards him. 'Here's your present.'

She was surprised. 'Mine?'

'You didn't suppose that you would be left out?' He sounded so astonished that she answered simply: 'I thought you might give me something off

the tree…' She waved a hand at a corner of the
room, where the tree, splendidly bedecked, stood,
waiting for the moment when its candles would be
lighted. Miss Thrums didn't like electric tree lights.

He shook his head at her and offered a gaily
wrapped box. 'Open it,' he laughed suddenly. 'It's
not the sapphires—they'll have to wait.'

She paused in her unwrapping to look up at him,
not sure if he was joking. But of course he was,
there was that funny bland look on his face; the
look he laughed behind when something amused
him. She opened the box. The golden angel, carefully wrapped in cotton wool, lay inside. Alexandra
took it out carefully and stood it on the hearth. 'Oh,
she's lovely!' she breathed. 'But it was only a joke,
you know…you shouldn't have…' She caught his
eye. 'Thank you very much, Doctor van Dresselhuys.'

'Taro.'

'All right—Taro.'

He bent down and wound the little figure up and
it began to revolve, tinkling out 'Away in a Man-
ger' with a faint sweetness, like a fairy playing the
piano. 'Oh,' said Alexandra, and smiled, 'it really
is Christmas, isn't it?' And then because he was
staring so hard: 'Should we not go to bed?' She got

to her feet. 'I'll clear this away in the morning—your room's quite ready.'

She bent to pick up the little angel and when she stood up again it was to find his arms encircling her. 'We'll have to imagine the mistletoe,' he said, and kissed her surprised mouth. 'Now go to bed.'

She went, the angel held delicately in one hand, not looking back. She didn't dare, he might have seen the look on her face; she was sure it was there; something must show of the surge of feeling tearing through her chest. She had never felt like this before—it was tremendous and exciting and surprising, probably it was because it was Christmas. She looked at the little angel cradled in her hand and knew that it wasn't anything to do with Christmas, indeed, it had nothing to do with the time of year. She supposed she would have fallen in love with Doctor van Dresselhuys at any season. She got ready for bed, wide awake now, sure that she wouldn't close her eyes all that night. She was wrong, of course, for no sooner had she laid her lovely head on the pillow than she was dreamlessly asleep.

She wakened early and remembered the tray and its contents scattered round the sitting-room fire, but when she crept downstairs, it was to find everything neatly tidied away, and early though it was, someone had been there to clear away the ashes and make a new fire, so she wasn't altogether surprised when the doctor bade her good morning from the kitchen, adding: 'And once more, a happy Christmas, my practical Miss Dobbs. Down early to clear up last night's little party, no doubt?'

She hadn't known how she would feel when she saw him; the uprush of delight was damped before she could enjoy it. She wished him a happy Christmas and good morning and considered what she should say next. But she had no need, for he went on blandly: 'You need not have worried, I always tidy up as I go.' He gave her a little mocking smile. 'I've made tea—would you like some?'

She was longing for a cup, but the idea of staying there while he made remarks like that at her was more than she could bear. 'No, thanks, but I'll take up a cup for Penny—she'll be down for breakfast this morning,' she smiled faintly, 'because you're here.'

He didn't answer her, only gave her a cup and saucer and told her to be careful not to spill it. She carried it upstairs very carefully, feeling hollow.

Everyone met half an hour later in the sitting-room, where the presents had been put round the tree. Breakfast, Miss Thrums had informed everyone, would be boiled eggs and toast, because church was at ten o'clock, and she had no intention of being late. As if by common consent, they waited for Penny to open her presents first. She sat by the fire with the little pile of parcels beside her, looking sweetly pretty, her cheeks coloured with excitement, her eyes sparkling, and as she opened each packet she thanked the giver charmingly—the scarf, the knitted gloves Miss Thrums had made after she had gone to bed each evening; the chocolates in their gay box, the bottle of perfume Alexandra had added just in case there weren't many presents. The bottom of the pile was a large box—a dress box, tied extravagantly with ribbon. Alexandra knew before it was opened what would be inside, and she was quite right: the blue dress. Penny squealed with delight and flung her arms round Taro and kissed him, and Alexandra, watching the indulgent smile on his face, wished with all her heart that she could wipe out Christmas Eve; that she had never stayed up to let the doctor in, that she had never discovered that she loved him…she remembered the little angel and swallowed tears.

'Oh, Penny, how super!' she cried gaily. 'You must wear it—just as soon as we're back from church.'

Penny looked mutinous. 'Oh, church,' she muttered. 'Taro, you're not going, are you?'

He was talking to his aunt. 'Of course I am, you silly child,' he told her carelessly over his shoulder, so that the mutinous look vanished and she skipped off to her room, the beautiful dress draped over her arms.

When she had gone, Miss Thrums said mildly: 'Well, you've made Penny very happy, Taro,' and looked as though she was going to say something more than that, but she didn't, only after a tiny pause she added: 'You have certainly made me very happy with my wheelbarrow—the pleasure I shall get from it…and did Alexandra get her sapphires?'

Alexandra avoided the doctor's eye. 'Something much nicer,' she declared, still determinedly gay, 'the little golden angel, no less. I'll fetch her for you to see.'

She whisked out of the room and upstairs—just a few moments to herself, that was all she wanted, she thought desperately. She stood in the centre of her little room and stared out of the window, making herself think about anything under the sun other than the doctor, and presently she went downstairs again, her gift cradled in her hand, her face as composed as it usually was. Perhaps she was a little pale, but no one would notice that.

They went to church in the Morris, and sang the Christmas carols, although Penny didn't sing them;

Alexandra, watching her covertly, came to the conclusion that she wasn't attending to the service at
all; she was thinking about something else. Yet she
could sing; Alexandra had heard her, joining in the
pop music on the radio, and she knew the words,
too. Probably her pretty head was full of the new
dress. Alexandra carolled away, thinking about that;
the doctor must have spent a good deal of money,
for besides the blue dress, which hadn't been much
under a hundred pounds, there had been a handful
of gay bangles, a leather purse, and a box of mar-
rons glacés. She allowed her gaze to slide sideways
to where he sat on the other side of Penny. He was
wearing a grey suit today, and as usual he was fault-
lessly turned out even though the clothes he was
wearing weren't new. She wondered what he had
gone without in order to buy his Christmas presents.

They went back to coffee and sherry and mince
pies; the turkey was already in the oven, the pudding steaming away in its saucepan. Alexandra
went away to lay the table and Penny disappeared
upstairs to come down very shortly in the new
dress. She looked lovely in it; Alexandra sup-
pressed envy as she admired it while Penny re-
volved and preened and then went to sit by the doctor; she could hear her gay chatter while she and
Miss Thrums saw to the dinner. Miss Thrums'

voice broke into her thoughts. 'That's what she needed, my dear—she's a changed girl, isn't she?'

Alexandra nodded. She had wound an apron round the jersey dress and her hair was becoming untidy; she pushed it back with an uneasy hand. 'I wonder if she has a brother or a boy-friend? She's so happy in the doctor's company.'

Miss Thrums gave the turkey a cautious prod and closed the oven door again. 'That seems to be working both ways,' she observed dryly. 'I don't think Taro expected quite so much youthful gaiety.'

'Oh, well—he'll enjoy it all the more, I daresay. Shall I dish up the sprouts?'

'Yes, my dear, and then get those two to the table, will you?'

Alexandra went just as she was, rather pink and shiny in the face, the apron still on, across the tiny hall and into the sitting-room. Penny and Taro were under the mistletoe, making, as far as she could see, very good use of it.

'I couldn't have come at a worse time, could I?' she exclaimed with false cheer, and when they turned to look at her: 'We do seem to interrupt each other at the wrong moment, don't we, Doctor?'

He wasn't in the least disconcerted, but then why should he be?—although Penny looked furious. 'Your aunt wants you at table so you can carve the turkey.' She turned to go again, aware that she must look pretty awful in her draped pinny and untidy hair, whereas Penny looked quite lovely; like someone on a chocolate box lid.

'Just a minute,' said Taro, and as she hesitated, broke a piece of mistletoe off the bunch above him and came across the room so fast that she had no chance to move. She managed to turn her cheek just a little, though, so that his kiss landed just below an eye. She wasn't sure why she had done it; perhaps because Penny was glaring at them. She met his smiling eyes and managed to smile too as he twirled her round and caught her arm. 'And now for Aunt Euphemia,' he declared, and made for the kitchen.

Penny would have liked to sulk during dinner, but none of them gave her the chance; the talk was gay and lighthearted and every now and then the doctor slipped in a question which might have led to a clue of some sort as to her past. But it was no good, they finished the meal without finding out anything which might help them, and afterwards he washed up, Alexandra's apron tied round his vast person, while Penny stayed close by, not helping at all, but keeping a jealous watch on all he did.

They did nothing much for the rest of the day. Penny declared that she was too tired to go for a walk—even in the garden, and Alexandra was wise enough to refuse the doctor's invitation to accompany him, although she longed to do so, and because Penny was showing signs of real temper by the evening, she spent more time than was really necessary getting their supper ready in the kitchen, attending to Rover and Sambo, and then devoted herself to Miss Thrums for the rest of the evening.

She told herself how silly she was as she got ready for bed; she could make rings round Penny if she wished to when it came to attracting a man, but somehow she couldn't do that, partly because Taro hadn't shown in any way that he would like her to. Christmas, she decided as she got into bed, was an overrated affair, and mistletoe was just plain silly.

They did go walking the next day, all four of them, with Rover trailing from side to side in a leisurely way so that they had to keep stopping to allow him to catch up with them. The doctor strode ahead with Penny beside him, no trace of her sulks apparent now. Only when he slowed down to join his aunt and Alexandra, who instantly partnered Penny, was it obvious that she was put out at his action. She walked along beside Alexandra, not bothering to answer any of her remarks, staring ahead with a face like a thundercloud, and presently

the doctor made matters even worse by joining
them with a careless: 'Keep Aunty company, will
you, Penny? I want to talk to Alexandra.'

It was only to discuss Penny's progress, they
could have been in the middle of a hospital ward
with a dozen people listening in, but it was only
too plain that Penny didn't think so. She barely
spoke to Alexandra for the rest of the day and went
to bed early, declaring that she had a headache. Her
temper wasn't improved by Taro's cheerful advice
to have a good sleep, and Alexandra, going upstairs
a little later to see how she felt, had her head bitten
off for her pains.

She was her charming self at breakfast the next
morning, though, and when Alexandra offered to
drive down to the village for the eggs Miss Thrums
always had from old Mrs Deed's hens, she offered
to go with her—something which astonished Alexandra very much, because the doctor was leaving
that afternoon and she had imagined that Penny
would want to spend every available moment with
him. He had offered to go himself, but it seemed to
her that he had had little enough opportunity to talk
to his aunt; there must be things they would wish
to discuss. She stifled a sigh as she went to get her
coat; it would have been marvellous to have had
him for company instead of Penny, but she put the

thought resolutely aside. She had promised herself not to think about him, even while she was quite well aware that to keep such a promise was quite beyond her powers. But at least she could try.

She made a grimace at her lovely reflection, jammed on her woollen cap and went downstairs, to find that Taro had brought the car round from the shed and was leaning on its bonnet, talking to Penny. They made a striking couple, she admitted to herself a little sourly.

It was on their way back, the eggs safely collected and in a basket on the back seat, that Penny, sitting beside Alexandra, chattering away quite amiably, suddenly leaned over and tried to wrench the wheel from her grasp.

The car swung across the road, hit a tree with its rear bumper, and lurched alarmingly before Alexandra managed to push Penny away, and with all her strength, regain control. And when Penny lunged forward once more, Alexandra slapped her hard, using her left hand while she hung on to the wheel with the other. She felt her palm slam into the other girl's cheek. 'Sorry, Penny,' she said in a voice a little shaky with fright, 'but I had to do that.'

She heard the girl whimpering beside her, but she didn't take her eyes off the road. It was empty, and a good thing too, she thought, putting her foot firmly down on the accelerator—the quicker they got back to the cottage the better. It came into sight round the next bend, and she heaved a sigh of relief; she was shaking now and a good burst of tears would have helped, but she turned the car into the short drive and stopped before the door and turned to Penny, so intent on asking what had come over her that she barely noticed the doctor and his aunt standing in the porch. But Penny had seen them; she was out of the car, running headlong into Taro's arms, sobbing incoherently, leaving Alexandra to follow her.

'Look what she did!' Penny's voice was a pitiful wail. 'She hit me—she went right across the road and drove into a tree and when I tried to steer for her, she hit me...'

Alexandra opened her mouth and then shut it again; Penny was having a brainstorm. In a few moments, when she was calmer, she would explain what had really happened.

'You hit her?' The doctor's voice was astonished.

'I slapped her—I had to...'

'Did it have to be quite so hard?' He wasn't astonished now, just coldly polite.

Alexandra looked at Penny—there was indeed a red mark on her cheek, but if she hadn't slapped her they might even now be in the ditch, the pair of them, with even worse injuries than a reddened cheek. She said again: 'It was necessary.'

'She was trying to make me remember,' said Penny, still in the same pitiful voice, 'and she got cross because I couldn't. She's damaged the car too, I heard it—I think it was the bumper.'

Miss Thrums had said nothing so far. 'Whatever happened,' she stated reasonably, 'I think it would be only fair to hear what Alexandra has to say— and would we not be more comfortable indoors?'

In the sitting room Alexandra took off her coat and watched the doctor performing the same office for Penny; he fetched something from his case too and attended to the fast disappearing patch on her cheek. He kissed it lightly when he had done and Alexandra choked back a snort of rage and turned her back; but only for a moment. Within seconds she faced them again, ready to give her explanation with calm reasonableness.

It was a pity that the doctor remarked, still very polite: 'You gave me to understand that you were a good driver.'

Sweet reasonableness flew out of her head and temper took over. 'Did I now? I must have got carried away, mustn't I?'

Impatience took over from politeness. 'There is no need to be flippant.'

'No?' Her voice, despite her best efforts, rose a little. 'What else should I be? Miss Thrums suggested that I might have something to say, but you aren't interested, are you?'

He answered her stiffly: 'I beg your pardon. I had every intention of asking you.'

'Pooh!' Her temper had risen nicely now, adding a sparkle to her eyes and a glow to her cheeks. 'I don't believe it, and since you've already decided to whom you're going to listen, I'll not take up another minute of your time. I'm sure you'll have no difficulty in finding someone with years of driving experience to take my place. I'm going to pack.'

She started for the door, to pause by Penny, still standing in the shelter of the doctor's arm. 'You had only to tell me that you didn't like me,' she told her quite gently. 'I would have gone without any fuss, you know—there was no need to go to such lengths…'

She made a dignified exit, shut the door quietly behind her and raced upstairs, where she packed with great speed and a sad lack of neatness, telling herself meanwhile that she was glad to be going, resolutely swallowing the tears she wouldn't allow herself to shed. It had all happened in a great hurry and perhaps she was being foolish; she didn't care, she had to get away from the house—and more than that, she had to get away from Taro, who didn't trust her.

CHAPTER FIVE

THERE was no one to be seen when she opened her bedroom door, and no sound. She peered over the stair rail and then went quietly down the hall, rather impeded by her suitcase. The hall was empty; she trod across it, suddenly aware that she would have to walk all the way to the village and hire its taxi. She was passing the closed door of the sitting room when it was opened and the doctor stopped her by putting a hand on her arm and at the same time taking her case from her and putting that on the floor behind him, which meant that to reach it she would have to push him to one side; a physical impossibility. So she stood still, looking past him. When he said: 'Alexandra, I'm sorry—will you come in here so that I can talk to you?' she lifted indignant eyes to his.

'No, I will not!' she declared firmly. A waste of breath; he lifted her gently off her feet and swung her round so that she found herself beside the case, and he shutting the door very gently behind her.

He said patiently: 'You're angry with me, and rightly so, but my dear girl, where is your tolerance, your womanly understanding? Put yourself in my place, confronted as I was by Penny in a state of hysteria, and you, looking like a ghost and shaking like a leaf.'

'I was not shaking like a leaf...'

'Oh, yes, you were.' His voice had been lightly mocking, but now it became harsh. 'You could have been killed.'

'Pooh—in that car? Doing a steady forty? Don't be melodramatic, Doctor van Dresselhuys.'

He looked as though he wanted to laugh. 'My dear good girl, you have this regrettable habit of saying "Pooh". But I don't wish to discuss your failings, rather your attributes.' He paused to run his eyes over her person. 'Your—er—nursing attributes. You have done Penny a great deal of good, and contrary to your impetuous conclusion, she likes you. Indeed, she has just told me that she has absolutely no recollection of any of the unfortunate happenings which occurred.'

Alexandra stared at him. 'Not remember?' she asked in amazement. 'But she said...you heard her.'

'I heard what she said, but she assures me that she can remember nothing at all—only that she found herself in this sitting-room.'

She was still staring at him, but she wasn't thinking about Penny at all. He was standing close to her, so close that she could, if she had a mind to, have leaned forward just a little and laid her head on his shoulder and had a good cry; it would have relieved her churned-up feelings splendidly. She spurned the thought and studied his face. He was undoubtedly the best-looking man she had ever seen, even when he was in a bad temper, but she didn't love him for his looks; she began to wonder what she did love him for...

'I suspect that your mind is not on the subject under discussion, Alexandra.' His voice was bland, but his eyes were intent. 'I wonder what you are thinking?'

It seemed best not to answer that; she said after a moment: 'What do you intend to do?'

'Ask you to go upstairs and unpack your things—beg you, if necessary, to stay.'

She knew then that she had been afraid that he would let her go; relief flooded over her, but all she asked was: 'You think that will really help?'

'Yes. Perhaps this afternoon's happenings were the tip of the iceberg; Penny acted without conscious thought, and we must help her all we can. Will you stay? Please, Alexandra?'

She gave him the briefest possible glance. There was no mockery or coldness in his face now. 'Very well,' she told him briefly, 'if you think it will be of some use. I'll take my case up to my room, or is there anything else you want to discuss? What about Miss Thrums' car? I'm afraid I've damaged it.'

'I'll deal with that, and I think the less we say about the whole matter the better, don't you agree? I shall be seeing Mr Thrush shortly; I believe the time has come to investigate Penny a little more fully—would you stay until that is done?'

He didn't wait for her answer but picked up her case and led the way back upstairs.

It was after he had gone that afternoon, while they were sitting round the fire, the three of them, that Alexandra allowed herself to think about Penny's strange behaviour in the car. The doctor had said that she had been unaware of what she had done, but she thought uneasily that that wasn't the case. She had seen Penny's eyes when she had tried to grab the wheel, and they had been the eyes of someone quite aware of what she was doing. And in that case, why had she done it?

During the days which followed, she could discover nothing which might help to solve the riddle. Penny acted towards her as she had always done— with a friendly, rather helpless manner which showed not the faintest hint of dislike. They went

for quite long walks together and into Needham
Market to shop and even, on the days when the
weather permitted, pottered in the garden; she had
never been so amenable, and Alexandra and Miss
Thrums congratulated each other on her progress
while they waited with outward patience for a word
from the doctor.

He arrived on New Year's Day, with Penny still
in bed and Alexandra and Miss Thrums busy in the
kitchen getting the breakfast, so that they were quite
unprepared for his sudden, silent appearance at the
kitchen door—at least Alexandra was; Miss Thrums
merely broke a number of eggs into the frying pan,
remarking: 'Ah, dear boy, there you are, how very
nice to see you again. Alexandra, you will have to
make a good deal more toast.' She put up her face
for his kiss and smiled at him before turning back
to the eggs.

Alexandra, cutting bread, avoided his eyes, afraid
that he might see her delight at his coming; she said
a quick: 'Hullo' and bent once more to her loaf.
Only when she had damped down her feelings did
she ask:

'Where on earth did you sleep? I thought the
ferry didn't get in to Harwich until about now.'

He leaned across the table and took a slice of
bread. 'There are other ways of getting here,' he

told her carelessly, and set about buttering his bread with a lavish hand. 'How's Penny?'

'Very well—happy too, isn't she, Miss Thrums?'

'Yes, dear. How very glad I am that you didn't go away—we should have been so uncomfortable with a stranger.' She looked round at her nephew. 'Have you been working hard, Taro?'

He bit into his slice. 'So-so, Aunty. I managed to see Thrush and we've come up with an idea between us. I'm going to take Penny back with me to Holland and get van Toller to have a look at her. You'll both come too, of course.' He smiled at them both in turn. 'This evening.'

His aunt dished up the eggs. 'What a splendid idea, Taro. When are we to go?'

Alexandra stopped cutting bread. She was a level-headed girl, but now she was startled. People—at least, the people she knew—didn't walk into a house at breakfast time and state that the household was to be uprooted in less than twenty-four hours. Of all the arrogance, she fumed silently—did he really suppose that she would meekly pack her bags and fall in with his high-handed wishes?

It seemed that he did, for as he leaned forward to take another slice of bread he remarked casually:

'I hope you're one of those people who keep their passports handy, Alexandra.'

'I do have it in my case,' she began, and then went on a little crossly: 'But don't imagine for one moment that I intend to be rushed into going abroad—talk about a moment's notice...' She drew a long, indignant breath. 'The very idea!'

'You're sounding off like a timid maiden lady, dear girl. Do remember that you're still young and healthy and—er—robust enough to take a small thing like an unexpected trip in your stride. I had no idea that you would carry on in this fashion.' He smiled at her with patient indulgence which made her even crosser. 'After all, Aunty hasn't turned a hair.'

'I am not your aunt,' Alexandra pointed out, 'and I'm not in a temper either.' She caught his eye and despite herself, burst out laughing.

'That's better.' He leaned over the table and kissed her on the end of her nose. 'And now what about breakfast, I'm famished.'

Alexandra, during that meal, allowed herself to be drawn into the discussion over their journey. She had taken up Penny's breakfast as usual, with strict instructions to say nothing about Taro's arrival or plans; now they sat round the kitchen table, making arrangements; at least, the doctor did the arranging,

Miss Thrums and Alexandra kept his cup and plate
filled and agreed meekly to what he had to say.
They would travel in the Morris, its bumper happily
repaired, and they would go by the night ferry from
Harwich.

'But where to?' asked Alexandra. 'It's all very
well, you know, but I haven't the slightest idea
where we're going; I simply must let my family
know.'

'Close to Leiden—that's about eleven miles from
The Hague—telephone your mother presently and
tell her that you'll telephone again as soon as we
arrive, you can give her the address then.'

Alexandra frowned. 'I haven't any clothes.'

She regretted the words immediately; he eyed her
up and down without haste, remarking blandly:
'Dear girl, there's a lot I could say in answer to
that, but I don't like to upset Aunty's sense of mod-
esty. Could you not buy what you need when we
get there? Contrary to your statement, I find, to my
disappointment, that you appear to be more than
adequately covered.'

'Taro,' said his aunt sternly.

'Dear Aunty, what have I said?' His voice held
all the innocence of a child. He looked at Alexandra, who was trying not to laugh. 'A dress, a coat,
things to go underneath them, shoes and stock-

ings—no, tights, isn't it? Something to cover your hair? You have all those things here, have you not?'

The two ladies exchanged a look. 'Men!' exclaimed Alexandra in disgust. 'They have no idea, have they?'

'None, my dear—although I do think that the clothes which you have with you should do very well.'

Her nephew beamed at her. 'Thank you, Aunty, I'm sure that Alexandra will listen to you.' He passed his cup for more coffee. 'That's settled, then. I'll tell Penny when she comes down, then I'd better go and have a look at the car.'

Alexandra, feeling swamped by circumstance, collected her wits. 'How long are we to be there?'

He looked vague. 'Who knows? Two weeks, three…it rather depends on van Toller.' He smiled at her. 'You don't know who he is, either, do you? A professor of Leiden Medical School—rather a well-known authority on amnesia. I'm hoping he'll have some ideas about Penny.'

Alexandra did her best to ignore the smile and asked matter-of-factly: 'But she hasn't a passport, has she? How can she go?'

'Oh, I've settled that. She'll be issued with a temporary one—I have to collect it on our way—special circumstances, you know.'

She didn't know, but she nodded. 'I can't speak Dutch,' she observed.

He laughed. 'What a girl you are for looking on the bright side! You won't need to, and if you should have to, I feel sure that you'll cope with our tiresome language with the same aplomb as you cope with everything else.'

'Thank you for your good opinion, Doctor van Dresselhuys.' She was aware that he had got his own way, which annoyed her. At the same time, the idea of accompanying him to his home was exciting; more than that, it had, she was bound to admit, driven every sensible thought from her head.

Later, of course, she came to her senses. She had been there when he had told Penny what he intended to do, and seen the girl's delight and his own smiling amusement at it, and had heard his reply when she had asked him if he were pleased to be taking her to his home. He had said: 'It is something I have been thinking about and planning, Penny,' and he had thrown an arm round her shoulders and smiled down at her, and Alexandra had been horrified at the strength of her own feelings as she watched. She had forced herself to think of other things, packing and getting the house ready to leave for a week or two; Miss Thrums had gone to a neighbouring friend with Sambo and Rover, and when she returned the doctor had busied himself looking over the car, and Penny had stayed with him, saying casually when she was asked if she would like to pack her things, that Alexandra could do it for her, and saying it so charmingly that there was nothing to do but go along to her room and put her few clothes into the case Miss Thrums had provided.

They had a late lunch and left before tea, for although there was no great distance to go, Penny's passport had to be collected in Ipswich. The doctor parked the car there, and he and Penny went off to see about it, leaving his aunt and Alexandra to find their way to the Great White Horse Hotel and order tea for the four of them. They came back in half an hour and Penny looked radiant.

Alexandra began to wish that she had never agreed to come; in the delightful anticipation of the doctor's company for the next week or so, she had almost convinced herself that he was only interested in Penny as a patient, but now she could see that she had been deluding herself—like a silly lovesick schoolgirl, she told herself disgustedly.

She accepted a cup of tea from Miss Thrums with a too bright smile, reflecting that life, at the moment, wasn't at all what she would wish it to be—in fact it hadn't been much fun for weeks now;

there had been Anthony to start with, she couldn't recall a single moment…she paused, a portion of muffin poised on her fork, suspended half-way to her mouth…there had; how could she have forgotten the cobweb morning? She smiled, remembering its brief enchantment, and became aware that Taro was looking at her. It was a disquieting look; searching and faintly amused, and yet somehow it conveyed the idea that he knew exactly what she was thinking. She just went on staring back at him, unable to think of anything to say to break the moment, and he made no effort to help her, although the amusement turned into a smile of such understanding that she might have said heaven knew what if Miss Thrums hadn't broken the spell with a prosaic remark about the tea they were drinking, so that Alexandra popped in the bit of muffin with the feeling that she had saved herself from appearing a fool, and that only at the very last minute.

They strolled round the town after tea and then drove on down to Felixstowe for dinner. The hotel at which they stopped was, Alexandra considered, far too grand—it would cost a fortune to pay for their meal, and one look at the menu confirmed her fears. She was hungry, for their lunch had been rather a snatched affair, and although she considered suggesting paying for herself, she decided against it, Taro would probably turn nasty if she did—unlike Anthony, she found herself thinking— so the only thing was to plead a lack of appetite and choose an omelette, which while doing very little to stay her hunger would at least reduce the bill by several pounds. She was glad that she had done so when Penny asked for the most expensive items on the menu, and the doctor, after a moment's hesitancy, chose an omelette for himself.

The ferry, when they boarded it, was half empty and Alexandra persuaded Penny to go to their cabin. 'An early night will do you good,' she coaxed. Penny was sitting on her bunk pulling off her clothes and tossing them around carelessly. 'What are you going to do?' She shot Alexandra a suspicious glance. 'Are you going back to talk to Taro?'

Alexandra took off her coat. 'No.' She had been entertaining that very idea. 'I'm coming to bed too.'

They went ashore after an early breakfast, and if Alexandra had expected the doctor to ask her why she hadn't joined him after seeing Penny to their cabin the night before, she was to be disappointed; he didn't mention it, merely hoped politely that they had both slept well and invited them to make a good breakfast before resuming his conversation with his aunt.

Penny, as was to be expected, demanded in the prettiest way imaginable to sit with Taro while he drove, which left Alexandra on the back seat with Miss Thrums. Not that she objected to this; she liked the lady very much; they got on very well together and she suspected that Miss Thrums was a good deal more observant than she appeared to be. She was an amusing talker too and embarked at once on a lively description of the country through which they were passing as they left the Hoek van Holland behind them.

It was still not quite light. The little town gave way to flat green fields, the ribbon of road running smoothly between them, the church spires of the next village already visible on the horizon. 'Monster,' Miss Thrums explained, 'a peculiar name, is it not? We turn off here so that we may avoid Den Haag. It's a pleasant road, running parallel to the motorway, and in a car such as this one, infinitely preferable. Our speed, you know.'

Alexandra nodded; the Morris was a splendid car but hardly built for competition with the Mercedes, Citroëns and Saabs which had come off the ferry. 'You know this road well?' she asked.

'Oh, dear me, yes. Taro brings me over on holiday at least twice a year—it makes a nice change.'

Alexandra thought of the dear little cottage they

had left; it would have to be something very special
indeed to make the change worthwhile. So far she
hadn't seen anything which particularly caught her
eye, although in all fairness she suspected that the
view she was looking at from the car window
wasn't a fair sample of rural Holland, an opinion
she changed very shortly, for there was a canal running alongside the road now and the green fields
had given way to patches of woodland.

'We're almost in Leiden,' Miss Thrums informed
her.

They drove through the heart of the little city and
Alexandra, oblivious of Penny's chatter, stared
around her. This was Holland as she had imagined
it; old houses with gabled roofs, tree-lined canals,
cobbled streets, and despite the spate of traffic, a
delightful air of not belonging to the twentieth cen-
tury at all, but still living in its glorious past. It was
disappointing that Taro didn't slow down at all, but
kept steadily on through the outskirts, across the
motorway and into a country road which presently
curved round an arm of water softened by trees.
They became thicker as they drove, with here and
there a clearing in which was set a small neat house
with one or two outbuildings, but these in turn gave
way to a high iron railing, painted black and gold-
tipped, enclosing what was undoubtedly the

grounds of a house, for there were smooth stretches of lawn, well arranged groups of trees and enough shrubs and flower beds to make the whole a colourful sight once winter had done with them.

'Now, that's a very pleasant place,' commented Alexandra, craning her neck to see as much of it as she could.

'I have always thought so,' agreed Miss Thrums. 'Each time I come here I realize how elegant it is.' As she was speaking the doctor had swung the car between two stone gateposts, into a smoothly gravelled drive which split in fifty yards or so, to encircle an ornamental pool with a little fountain in its centre before opening on to a big sweep before the house. It was of a comfortable size, of stone painted white and with a large porch supported by pillars. The front door was painted a glossy black, as were the frames of the large windows, and running across the face of the house above them was a wrought iron balcony with similar large windows opening on to it. A satisfying, comfortable house and meticulously maintained. Alexandra looked in vain for peeling paint and shabbiness; if this was Taro's house, then it didn't fit in at all well with his comfortable old tweeds and the Morris 1000. She was on the point of forming a carefully worded question when Penny forestalled her. 'Is this yours,

Taro?' She was very excited. 'Do you mean to say that you live here? It's enormous!' Her eyes were everywhere, taking everything in. 'You must be...'

He interrupted her smoothly: 'This is my home, yes. Shall we go in and have coffee before we do anything else?'

The door opened as they reached it and an elderly man, rather portly, greeted the doctor, bowed slightly to the rest of the party and ushered them into the hall. 'This is Pieters,' said Taro, and smiled at him. 'Here is my aunt again, as you see, and this is Sister Dobbs.'

Alexandra shook hands and said how do you do because Taro had spoken English and obviously Pieters must know some at least, but Penny, when it was her turn, merely nodded her head in an off-hand way and made no effort to shake Pieters' hand, so that Alexandra wondered uneasily that she had done the right thing and then decided that she had; it was Penny who had been a little rude, but unintentionally so, she felt sure.

They walked across the hall, a spacious place with white-painted walls and a staircase opposite the door, its wings disappearing left and right to the floor above. A little behind the others, Alexandra looked around her. The furniture was old and beautifully cared for, the pictures on the walls were mostly oil paintings, dim portraits and wintry land-scapes, and the ceiling had some splendid plaster-work. She followed the others through an arched double door and paused again to take stock of her surroundings. The sitting-room, perhaps? Though it was splendid enough to be a drawing-room—whichever it was it was large and lofty enough to accommodate ten times their number and very com-fortable besides, with great armchairs and sofas and small tables, bearing delicate porcelain reading lamps and silver bits and pieces. There was a great display cupboard along one wall and thickly cush-ioned window seats, exactly right to curl up on with one of the books housed in the revolving bookcase at the other end of the room, and just to complete the picture there was a bull terrier coming across the thick carpet to meet them and behind him, two nondescript cats. But she couldn't linger by the door any longer, she joined the others, and when the doctor invited her to sit down, did so, listening to Penny's excited comments and giving polite an-swers to Miss Thrums' sensible ones. To Taro she spoke not at all, and that was made easy by the fact that he didn't address her.

They drank their coffee from delicate china borne in on a massive silver tray by Pieters. Penny com-mented upon these too and even essayed a guess at the value of the tray, a remark which sent Miss Thrums' eyebrows up and caused a faint look of distaste to pass over the doctor's features, but it was only there for a second, he was laughing at her exuberant spirits before Alexandra could be sure that it had been there at all.

'You would like to go to your rooms, I expect,' he declared presently. 'Aunty, will you take Penny up to the little room at the end of the back corridor? I'll see Pieters about the luggage.' And when Alexandra made to follow them: 'Not you, Miss Dobbs—a word with you, if you please.'

He had spoken so quietly that the others, not hearing, were already crossing the hall towards the staircase. She felt her heart quicken, probably he was only going to give her instructions about Penny, but even that would make a nice change from the few polite utterances he had made during the morning. She sat down again, looking, she hoped, composed.

The doctor didn't sit down, but took up his position before the brightly burning fire in the wide hearth, with Butch, the dog, beside him. He said on a laugh: 'You are surprised, Alexandra?'

'Yes,' she answered baldly, and then cried impulsively: 'And to think I chose an omelette!'

Only for a moment was he puzzled, then he let

out a great bellow of laughter. 'Oh, my delightful Miss Dobbs—I wondered what had happened to your appetite, but I supposed you to be nervous of the crossing. How kind and thoughtful of you—I cannot call to mind any one of my acquaintances who would have given my financial state a thought when ordering their dinner at my expense.'

This annoyed her and she said with a decided snap: 'Naturally they wouldn't, they knew that you could afford it—I didn't.' She cast him a lowering look and was further annoyed to find him smiling.

'You do not approve, my dear Miss Dobbs?'

'Of you pretending to be poor? Or that you have a lovely house?' She tried to make her voice cool and reasonable. 'It's no business of mine, Doctor; I'm only here on a job.'

He was still smiling. 'I'm not aware that I ever led you to suppose that I was a poor man. You're quite put out, aren't you, dear girl? Perhaps it would be best if we continue our talk later, I daresay you're tired, but there is something...' He became all at once businesslike.

'Penny—she is to see Professor van Toller in two days' time. I shall be very interested...' he paused. 'I had thought, once or twice—perhaps you hadn't noticed?' He gave her an inquiring, wholly professional look.

'Yes, I had.'

He nodded in satisfaction. 'A foolish question to ask, I beg your pardon. But not enough to go on, is there?'

'No.' She had a sharp recollection of Penny taking the wheel from her and the look of complete awareness in her blue eyes, but he had never asked her about that afternoon, and since he obviously considered her to have been the one at fault, she had no intention of telling him now. Besides, telling him would make no difference now. She glanced round the lovely room and tried to imagine Penny living in it, for undoubtedly that was what she intended to do; her attitude towards Taro had become slightly proprietorial since their journey had begun, she must feel very sure of him, and he wasn't such a fool that he couldn't see that for himself. He wanted it, of course; a vivid memory of his white and angry face as Penny had rushed out of the car and into his arms made Alexandra feel a little sick and her heart twisted painfully. She wondered, not for the first time, why he had wanted her to come. Surely Miss Thrums could have managed, and in a house of this size there would be plenty of help. Her unspoken thought was answered just as though she had uttered it aloud.

'I want Penny to get out and about; nothing too

violent in the way of exercise, but walking—you ride? Yes? There are a couple of good mounts, but I fancy she doesn't ride. And no driving,' he added, and Alexandra, who had been regarding him with love, felt her temper rise. So she wasn't to drive! Now perhaps would be the time to explain about that afternoon, after all, but his gentle: 'You wouldn't be safe, dear girl,' struck her dumb with rage.

She had better get away before she exploded. As she got to her feet she asked: 'There's nothing more? Perhaps I might go to my room now.'

He shot her an unsmiling look. 'Of course, I'll get Nel to take you up.' He pulled the bell rope hanging beside the hearth and when a pleasant-faced middle-aged woman came, gave her some instructions and then turned to Alexandra. 'You took an instant exception to me when we met,' he observed in a contemplative voice. 'That must be overcome, though I must admit that I find it hard going.' He smiled suddenly. 'And now go upstairs and wash off that cross face, Alexandra. We lunch at half past twelve.'

CHAPTER SIX

IF Nel hadn't been there, beaming at them both,
Alexandra might have answered him back; instead
she followed the woman out of the room and up
the staircase, along an arched gallery overlooking
the hall and into a room which rather took her
breath. It overlooked the gardens at the side of the
house and although it wasn't very large, it had the
same high ceiling as the room downstairs and the
same painted walls. It was furnished quite beautifully in the Regency style, and Alexandra, explor-
ing once she was left on her own, saw that the bed
and the small table in the window were antiques,
as was the bow-fronted chest against one wall and
the little button-backed crinoline chair standing in-
vitingly beside the burnished steel grate. There
seemed to be no particular colour scheme; pinks
and blues and pale greens were nicely harmonized
in the curtains and bed cover, and the floor was
covered by a deeply piled white carpet. Very cosy,
she decided, aware that this was an understatement.
There was a small bathroom leading out of the bedroom too, all pink and white and containing every-

thing she could possibly want. She eyed it with deep pleasure and went back into the room to unpack and do her face and hair and presently went in search of Penny.

She met Miss Thrums first, however, for that lady flung open a door on the opposite side of the gallery and invited her to enter. This room was delightful too, larger and more splendidly furnished and facing the ornamental pool.

'Very comfortable, isn't it, my dear?' murmured Miss Thrums, 'and so different from my cottage. It always surprises me that when Taro comes to stay with me he gets the morning tea and peels the potatoes as though he had done such things all his life. I daresay if he attempted to do either of these things here, his devoted staff would be appalled.'

She took a look at Alexandra. 'You were surprised? I don't suppose Taro thought of telling you, you see, he wouldn't have considered it important.' She paused. 'And it isn't, is it, Alexandra—not to you.'

'No. I think I—I felt sorry for him at first, you see he wore those tweeds—nice but shabby—and he was driving the Morris; I quite thought it was his. I imagined him to be a GP with not too much money and perhaps a wife and children...'

'Too much money, my dear,' declared Miss

Thrums, 'and no wife—he hasn't had time to look for one yet, or so he says.' She shot another look at Alexandra. 'But I'm wondering if he'll have to look much further.'

Alexandra turned to look out of the window. 'Probably not,' she said in a colourless voice, and thought of Penny. Which reminded her to say: 'I think I'd better go along and see if Penny has unpacked. Is her room nearby?'

'Across the front corridor and down the little passage at the back,' directed her companion. 'Did Taro tell you at what time we lunch?'

'Yes, thank you, I'll see you then.'

Penny hadn't unpacked; she was lying on the little canopied bed, her kicked-off shoes on the thick floral-patterned carpet, her coat tossed carelessly over a chair. She wasn't asleep either, for when Alexandra went in she turned her head to look at her.

'I say, Alexandra, isn't this great? All this.' She waved an expressive arm. 'I had no idea, had you? He must be rolling in lolly—and to think I didn't guess!' She smiled happily and her blue eyes weren't just aware now, they were secretive too. 'I can twist him round my little finger,' she said in a dreamy, satisfied voice. 'I discovered how to do that years ago...' She put a hand up to her mouth in a swift, guarded movement and then went on quickly: 'At least, I imagine I did, though I've no way of remembering, have I—it's terrible not to know anything.'

Alexandra's face displayed nothing of her feelings. 'It must be,' she answered pleasantly, 'but I daresay the specialist you're to see will be able to help you.'

She fancied Penny looked apprehensive. 'What will he do?'

'Ask you questions, I expect. I don't know much about it, but these people can get at your subconscious mind and help you to remember. Think how wonderful it will be if he brings your memory back, Penny—you'll be able to go back to your family.'

She watched Penny's face and tried to decide whether the expression upon it was fear, anger or excitement; it was impossible to tell.

'What about getting some of your things tidied up?' she asked briskly, 'and getting ready for lunch.'

They went downstairs presently and found the doctor and his aunt sitting together by the fire, drinking sherry, and when he had fetched their drinks he went back to his chair again, only Alexandra saw him turn it slightly so that he could watch Penny, who, on entering the room, had be-

come small and defenceless and amusing in a little
girl fashion. Behaviour nicely calculated to catch
any man's eye, and the doctor, Alexandra noted
crossly, had certainly been caught. Watching
Penny, she had to admit that she was very clever;
it was impossible to imagine her to be the same
little virago who had tried so hard to make her ditch
the car and who had lain on her bed not half an
hour earlier and allowed her to see so clearly that
she intended to get Taro—and she had almost given
herself away…or had she? Perhaps she was doing
the girl an injustice. She sighed, caught Taro's eye
and smiled a brilliant smile to let him see that she
was enjoying herself hugely.

They lunched in a small room, oak-panelled and
with small windows overlooking the grounds at the
back of the house. They sat at a round oak table,
on tall carved chairs, and there was little else in the
room save a vast sideboard and a great bowl of
flowers on an exquisite china pedestal.

Alexandra loved it, but Penny exclaimed in disappointment: 'Oh, is this the dining-room? I
thought it would be much larger and grander. There
aren't any pictures,' her eyes swept the sideboard,
'and no silver.'

'What did you expect?' asked the doctor in a
tolerant voice, 'gold plate and footmen? But if it

will make you any happier, there is another dining-room; it's too large for us.'

'Do you give parties—big ones?' Penny had waved the soup away impatiently.

'Occasionally—when I have reason to celebrate something.'

She smiled bewitchingly. 'Then we can have one while I'm here, can't we? Oh, Taro, please!'

'Let's be practical,' he begged her, half laughing. 'I'm a hard-working doctor. The time I've wasted rushing to and fro to check up on you is no one's business, and somehow I've got to make that time up. No party, Penny.'

She pouted prettily. 'Taro, not even a teeny one? Then we'll have to do something to make up for it. Couldn't we go out to dinner and go to a theatre? Surely there's a theatre or a night club?'

The doctor's expression didn't change, he applied himself to the canard à l'orange with which Pieters had just served him. 'You seem to have had quite a taste for the bright lights,' he observed lightly, 'you must have been a swinger that past life of yours.'

He barely glanced at her before he turned to his aunt. 'I've one or two appointments,' he told her. 'If I'm delayed I'll telephone, but I should be back by seven o'clock—if I'm not, don't wait dinner.'

He glanced at Alexandra. 'The library is on the other side of the hall, do take any book you want,' he told her pleasantly, 'and might I suggest that you and Penny go for a brisk walk before tea? And that's at half past three, by the way. There's a very small village about half a mile down the road, the church is rather quaint. Pieters will tell you how to get the key if you want to go inside, he speaks a little English and understands a great deal.'

He left them almost immediately after they had finished lunch, and Alexandra, standing idly by the window while Penny and Miss Thrums finished their coffee, wasn't really surprised when she saw the car he drove himself away in—a silver-grey Rolls-Royce, no less. Nothing else would have done, she conceded, watching its sleek nose slide past the corner of the house. He looked up as he passed and waved, and even as she returned this salute she felt annoyance at herself for being at the window in the first place. He had waved just as though he had expected her to be there, too. He would think her vulgarly curious. She joined the others without mentioning the Rolls; Penny would find out soon enough.

They went to get their coats shortly afterwards and Penny was so sweet and charming during their walk that Alexandra became full of doubt once more. She really shouldn't have the job at all, she thought worriedly; the fact that she was in love with Taro herself made her most unsuitable and probably she was imagining things about Penny just because of it. The poor girl needed someone older and more motherly, someone who would listen with kindly tolerance to her ceaseless chatter about the doctor. Perhaps she really was in love with him, thought Alexandra, leaning over backwards to be tolerant and motherly, although she didn't think so; Penny was enchanted with his good looks and his deep voice and his beautiful house and unexpected wealth, but then she herself was enchanted too, not that she cared a button whether he had any money or not; he would do very nicely just as he was, thought Alexandra longingly, and never mind the trimmings.

But being woeful about it wasn't going to help at all, she was on a job and just because she was in love with the doctor was no reason to be suspicious of Penny. She laid herself out to be as nice as she could to her charge for the rest of the day; it was rather a strain, especially when after dinner, Penny knelt at the doctor's feet, gazing adoringly into his face. The fact that he was, for the greater part of the time, deeply immersed in some papers and quite unaware of this made very little difference, made it no easier to watch. Even when he looked up briefly and asked her what she thought of the newest twinbagged catheters, his question was uttered in such an impersonal tone—just as though they had been standing in the recovery room—that she took no pleasure from it, and mumbled a reply quite lacking in observation, earning nothing more than a raised eyebrow on his part. She didn't see him at all the next day; he was away before eight o'clock and she had been in bed an hour or more when she saw the lights of the car from her bed. By listening hard she could just make out the purr of the Rolls passing beneath her window. A long day, she thought sleepily; he would be tired out. Probably Pieters or Nel or the plump Bet who did the cooking would be waiting up to get him a meal. She sat up and thumped her pillows, wide awake again, and then froze at the tap on her door. It was Pieters' voice, very low, which reached her ear, urging her in his basic English to put on a robe and go downstairs.

She was out of bed, tearing into her dressing gown and thrusting her feet into her slippers almost before he had finished speaking; Taro must be ill—unconscious—dying, perhaps. She raced downstairs, hair flying, her face a picture of fear, and plunged through the door Pieters was holding open for her.

Taro was sitting at the table, a bowl of soup before him, a glass in his hand. He looked the picture of good health, albeit a little tired, and she skidded to a halt half-way across the room to protest: 'I thought you were ill—or something frightful. Pieters said come downstairs…' She fetched a breath. 'I was in bed,' she added accusingly.

He had got to his feet, watching her. 'So I see,' he spoke on a laugh, 'and very nice too; the hair is very pretty like that, you should wear it hanging down your back.'

She felt bewildered; surely she hadn't come downstairs at that hour of night to discuss hair styles with him. 'Don't be absurd—I'm not a girl.'

'No? I beg to disagree about that.' He smiled so nicely that she almost smiled back at him, but remembered in time to ask severely: 'Is it urgent? Whatever it was you wished to see me about?'

For answer he pulled out the chair beside his. 'Come and sit down, Pieters shall bring you something—coffee, perhaps?—then I can finish my supper with a clear conscience. You see, I have to leave at six o'clock tomorrow morning and I haven't yet told you where to go with Penny.' He began on his soup. 'She's to be at van Toller's rooms at half past ten. Pieters will drive you in and Aunty will be with you. I'll meet you there and when it's finished, I'll drive you both back. Aunty wants to do some shopping and come back with Pieters later.' He glanced at her. 'Is that clear?'

The coffee had come and she poured herself a cup while Pieters set a grilled steak before the doctor. 'Yes, thank you. When shall we know the results of—of whatever is going to be done?'

She thought how guarded his face looked. 'Perhaps at once. It's a gamble.'

'Isn't that rather soon?'

'Not in certain circumstances—you see, we think we know what the result will be.'

She chose her words carefully. 'Would it make any difference to you whatever it is? I mean, supposing Penny isn't likely to regain her memory ever again?—That can happen with retrograde amnesia, can't it? Would it matter very much?'

'You are referring, I imagine, to my personal feelings. It won't make a scrap of difference to me, either way.'

The coffee cup before her became a little misty and she couldn't quite trust her voice. She gulped the scalding liquid instead and choked—providentially—because now it didn't matter that tears filled her eyes. He thumped her back gently, proffered his handkerchief and refrained from commenting on the super-abundance of tears on her cheeks. When she had recovered a little, he went on with his supper until she asked: 'How long is Penny to stay here? That is, if nothing more can be done?'

She waited anxiously for his answer, and when it came she was disappointed; he was going to tell her nothing. 'Ask me that question after she has seen van Toller,' he advised her lightly. 'There's an excellent pudding, you'd better have some of it.'

'But I had dinner…'

'I shall be lonely if you go.'

She assented weakly, eating her share of the castle puddings, light as air, which Pieters had placed before them, and then having another cup of coffee while Taro drank his. And gradually she relaxed under the gentle flow of his small talk, and presently she found herself telling him about her home and parents. 'Though Miss Thrums' cottage is just as pretty as Father's house,' she told him, 'it's like a fairytale house. Did you really mean that—that you would like a home just like hers?' She turned to look at him inquiringly. 'I don't see how you could have when you have all this.'

'Oh, make no mistake. I love this place down to the last bolt and nail, but it would be very pleasant to have a small place to go to,' he gave her a wicked look, 'where I could wear old clothes and saw logs and walk instead of driving.'

'You can do all that here.'

He shook his head. 'I seldom have the time. Were you sorry for me, Alexandra?'

'Well, yes. You see, I thought the Morris was yours and that's hardly a successful doctor's car, is it, and your clothes were—well, the old ones you liked wearing, I suppose, but I didn't know that, did I? And when you visited Miss Thrums, you never came in a car—I thought you had to walk from the nearest bus stop.' She gave him a defiant look. 'Now tell me I'm silly, you must have thought it often enough.'

He said slowly: 'No, dear Miss Dobbs, I have never thought that of you; nothing you could do or say would alter my opinion of you. And now I think that perhaps you had better go to bed,' and when she got obediently to her feet, he got up too and kissed her gently on her cheek before going to open the door for her. She looked down as she reached the head of the stairs and he was still standing there, watching her.

She did as he had told her in the morning, coaxing Penny, who quite suddenly didn't want to go to see a specialist, to get up and dress and eat some sort of a breakfast. Somehow she managed to have her ready by the time Pieters came to the door, sitting in the driving seat of a BMW 520.

They were met in the hall by Miss Thrums, clad, as was her wont, in a sensible tweed coat and a felt hat which could only be described as vintage. She exchanged an understanding glance with Alexandra and declared her intention of sitting in front with Pieters, leaving her the task of keeping Penny happy during the short drive.

Professor van Toller lived close to the Rapenburg Canal, in a tall thin house in the middle of a row of houses exactly similar. He was a burly man, giving the impression that at any moment he would split the seams of his well cut suit; he must have a good tailor, thought Alexandra, shaking hands and warming at once to his fatherly manner. But Penny, when she was introduced to him, hung back a little and when, after a few minutes' aimless talk, he suggested that he might start his examination, she declared that she wouldn't be examined and that no one could force her, a state of affairs happily put right by the appearance of Taro, looking somehow quite different—remote and professional—in his sober grey suit. He overrode her objections in a friendly, compelling manner which gave her no chance at all, and Professor van Toller's nurse opened his consulting room door. He ushered

Penny in, exchanged a look with Taro and turned
to Alexandra. 'I think it would be as well if you
were present, Miss Dobbs—instead of my own
nurse, you know.' He swept her inside too, with
Taro behind her, and she thought she knew why he
had done it; it would be nicer for Penny, for a start,
and all doctors liked a nurse or secretary there when
they were dealing with young women, they were
useful to help with the taking off and putting on of
clothes and they were reassuring. She took the chair
Taro nodded her into, and waited.

Professor van Toller seated himself behind his
desk and glanced at the papers before him. 'Retrograde amnesia,' he rumbled to himself. 'Now,
young lady, let me see...' He muttered his way
through the notes, occasionally asking a question,
and referring at times to Taro, speaking with a word
of apology, in their own language. Presently he laid
the notes down and sat back, just looking at Penny,
who at first looked back at him and then presently
dropped her eyes. Alexandra, uncomfortably aware
of tension in the air, was taken completely by surprise when he said suddenly: 'And now, Miss
Dobbs, we will hear your precise account of what
happened while you were driving the car.'

She didn't look at Penny or Taro. 'Penny has
already told Doctor van Dresselhuys that she can't

remember anything about it—is it really necessary? No harm was done…'

'Very necessary, Miss Dobbs. You have not been asked to tell your version of this occurrence for several good reasons. If you will begin, please.' He beamed at her. 'I listen attentively,' he assured her.

'Well,' she began slowly, and was interrupted by Penny.

'She'll tell you a lot of lies,' she said rapidly. 'She doesn't like me, and I'll tell you why…'

She was interrupted in turn by Taro with a swift smoothness which gained Alexandra's instant admiration. 'Penny,' he said quietly, 'it would be wise for you to hold your tongue,' and his tone was such that she did so at once, her blue eyes on his face; a questioning look, tinged with suspicion.

Alexandra made her statement as briefly as possible and when she had finished, the professor asked: 'And your own impression, Miss Dobbs?'

She looked at Penny. 'I'm sorry,' she told her quietly, and then turned back to Professor van Toller. 'I may have been mistaken, but at the time I had the impression that Penny was quite aware of what she was doing, and I don't think that she had forgotten it when we got back to Miss Thrums' house.'

'And other than that, have you at any time been

given cause to wonder if this young lady's amnesia was complete?'

'Once or twice.'

'You will be good enough to tell us.'

'The first time was a few weeks ago, the second time was the day before yesterday.'

'And?'

'I would rather not repeat the conversation. Would you just take my word for it?'

The professor beamed again. 'For the moment, Miss Dobbs. And now let us take a look at our patient.' He spoke to the room at large. 'Hypnosis might serve us very well in this case—to obtain information from the patient's subconscious and feed it back to her, as it were. It has been known to prove successful in a number of cases.' He looked around him. 'Now, I shall want that powerful lamp just here, I think, and if the young lady will sit...'

'I won't—it's a trick!' shouted Penny. 'You're only leading me on. You know—you knew all the time,' she turned furiously to Alexandra. 'And you, spying on me, trying to catch me out, listening and smiling. When did you start to guess, eh? But I was too clever for you—and now you're telling lies because you don't want me to win, do you?' She laughed. 'It was so funny, you knew what I wanted, didn't you, and you wanted the same thing, but you couldn't do anything about it—and that silly old woman…'

'You will leave my aunt out of this.' Taro's voice was coolly professional. 'You will also stop abusing Miss Dobbs. You will tell us your name and family details, and I advise you to tell the truth, for we can check it easily enough.'

'How long have you known?' demanded Penny sullenly. 'You never let on…'

'I suspected that your amnesia wasn't genuine some time ago, but I had no positive proof, and in any case it was necessary for you to be seen by another doctor before my suspicions could be confirmed. You would never have told us, would you, Penny?'

'Take me for a fool? Well, now what am I supposed to do?'

'Your name?' prompted the professor.

She said sulkily: 'Jacqueline Coster. I'm twenty-three, my home's in Birmingham—leastways, Mum and Dad live there, I haven't seen them for a couple of years—longer than that. I live with a boy-friend in London. We had a tiff and I walked out on him and hitchhiked—got that car from a chap I know; he said he'd borrowed it. I was having a ride round when I hit trouble.'

'Why didn't you tell us this as soon as you re-membered it?' Taro's voice was impersonally kind.

'Think I'm soft?' Penny laughed. 'I was on to an easy life, wasn't I? I had my plans too, and when we got here...' She paused. 'What are you going to do?'

'Send you home, Penny. You will have to make a statement to the police because you're still on their books as a case to be solved. You will be taken to the airport, I should imagine, and accom-panied to England by one of our policewomen. When you're in England you will be able to decide where you wish to go. Your parents will be told, of course, and so, if you wish, will your boy-friend. And now if you will wait in the other room, the professor and I have one or two things to discuss.'

The two of them sat uneasily looking out of the window. Alexandra had tried to talk, but Penny hunched a shoulder and turned away. It was fortu-nate that the two men were only a few minutes, and when the professor had wished them good-bye, Taro suggested to Alexandra's astonishment, that they might have lunch before they went back. 'There's a good restaurant close by,' he told them, and took Penny's arm, leaving Alexandra to follow them out into the street.

It was surprising, but lunch was a success; Taro

made no mention of Penny's leaving, there was certainly no reproach in his manner towards her, and after the first few awkward minutes she had reverted to her charming air of helplessness. The girl was a splendid actress, decided Alexandra, spearing sole Montreuil; the food was delicious, but she had no appetite, and although she contributed her share of the conversation when necessary, she left the other two to do the talking. It was three o'clock when they got into the Rolls, and Pieters was crossing the hall with the tea tray as they reached the house. Miss Thrums was at home; she greeted them with her normal brisk manner as they went into the sitting-room, poured tea, asked their opinion of Leiden, and pointed out, rather obviously, that it was beginning to snow, evincing not the least curiosity as to what had happened that morning. Only when they had finished tea did she suggest that Penny might like to pack her things. 'And I'll come with you,' she declared, blandly oblivious of Penny's mutinous expression. 'Packing is such a dull undertaking on one's own.'

Alexandra waited for Penny to object, but she didn't; she followed Miss Thrums meekly from the room, only pausing by Taro to ask: 'Taro, please may I talk to you when I come down? I'll only be a few minutes.'

Her smile, when he agreed, was exactly right—apologetic, sweet and appealing.

Alexandra sitting by the fire still, said nothing—indeed, she could think of nothing to say. Presumably she would be given the polite sack very shortly; she had half expected to be sent back with Penny—perhaps the doctor was about to do it now. She looked at him inquiringly and he smiled.

'Do you find me hard-hearted?' he asked her. 'I could think of no other way of getting her to own up—besides, I could have been mistaken; the amnesia could have been genuine.'

'It must have been very difficult for you,' Alexandra agreed soberly, 'and horrid too. I'm sorry—perhaps when everything's settled, you could meet Penny again.'

His surprise was absolute; it was a pity that she wasn't looking at him and didn't see it. It gave way to amusement almost immediately and when she did look up it was to see a faint smile round his mouth. 'Do you think I should?' he inquired of her.

'Well, it's nothing to do with me, but I imagine one's feelings don't change...especially when one had already guessed...and when one's happiness...' She came to a halt, bogged down in ones.

'Ah, yes, of course,' said her companion, 'then one must do something about it, mustn't one?'

She cast him an annoyed look. 'There's no need to mock me,' she pointed out sharply. 'You've always done that.'

'It's called defensive action,' he murmured. 'Alexandra, I have to go back to Leiden—a patient—I shall be half an hour or so, no longer, for I want to be here when Penny leaves. If someone comes for her before I get back will you ask them to wait and telephone me? Better still, tell Pieters to do that. But I should be back in ample time. This evening I think we might have a talk, there is a lot I want to say to you.'

About Penny? Certainly he would give her notice. She said calmly: 'Oh, yes, about me going.'

'No, it's not...' He would have said more, but the door opened and Penny came in. Alexandra could see by her face exactly what she planned to do; she didn't think the doctor would change his mind, but one could never be sure and Penny could be very beguiling—and Taro was a rich prize. Penny looked prettier than ever and very defenceless; Alexandra didn't wait to see any more but slipped out of the room with the girl's plaintive, 'Oh, Taro...' ringing in her ears.

She was in her room making tentative efforts to get her things ready to pack at a moment's notice when she heard Penny coming up the staircase. She was crying heartbrokenly and muttering to herself, so that Alexandra threw down a pile of undies and dashed out, intent on comforting her, but Penny ran down the passage to her room and locked the door behind her and no amount of knocking would persuade her to open it. Alexandra gave up presently and started back to her own room where she found Miss Thrums standing in her doorway. She said calmly: 'Don't worry, my dear, she's a very excitable girl, isn't she? I've been expecting something like this, and so have you. Taro hadn't time to tell me much, but what he hasn't told I think I have guessed, and now she's been trying to charm him into letting her stay. I really believe that she thought it would be a—walkover. It would be useless, of course, if she had known him better, she would never have attempted to make him change his mind.' She stood aside. 'Come in for a few minutes and talk to me. I must admit that I am upset about the whole business, although it hasn't come as a complete surprise to me—one has a sixth sense, perhaps. Taro will be back shortly and Penny will stay in her room until he does.'

She was quite wrong. Neither she nor Alexandra heard Penny's soft descent of the staircase. She was carrying her coat and a zipper bag, empty, under one arm.

It was quite ten minutes later when Pieters knocked on the door. 'It's the Miss,' he said hesitantly. 'Five minutes ago I see her walking to the gate at the back. She has a bag and Butch on his lead. Perhaps it is in order, but it seems not right.' He looked from one to the other. 'The bag is moving,' he added in a puzzled voice.

Alexandra had got out of her chair. 'Pieters, did you hear Miss Penny say anything? Earlier perhaps, when she came upstairs?'

His mild blue eyes widened. 'Yes, Miss Dobbs—she speaks with the doctor and comes upstairs. I do not understand everything but it was: "I will make him remember—I will pay…"'

The two ladies exchanged glances. At the door Alexandra said: 'I'll get my coat and find her. Pieters, have you seen the cats?'

It seemed a silly question. 'No, miss. Their plates stand ready in the kitchen, but they are not there—that is not as usual.'

She was on the way downstairs, putting on her coat as she went. She wasn't sure, but she thought she knew where Penny had gone and what she was going to do. There was a canal beyond the lane at the back of the grounds and she had Butch with her, and Alexandra was willing to bet her month's salary that the cats were in the zipper bag. They were going to be Penny's payment.

CHAPTER SEVEN

RUNNING was hazardous, but run Alexandra did, with all possible speed, slipping and stumbling first on the short turf and then on the icy lane, made more treacherous by the light powdering of snow falling from a dull grey sky.

But she had one advantage, her progress was almost silent, and she was on the rough little path leading to the canal before Penny heard her. She was kneeling down, tying a rusty iron bar to Butch's lead—left lying about by some fool, thought Alexandra wildly, while beside her in the zipper bag, Nibbles and Kiki chorused fearfully, but when she saw Alexandra she dropped the bar and picked up the bag. Alexandra, on the bank now, unzipping her boots and ripping off her coat, saw the little eddy of muddy water rise to the surface as it was flung into the canal.

The cats first, she thought incoherently; if she were quick—and lucky—she would be in time to save Butch as well; the iron bar would take some fastening and he wouldn't be easy to heave into the water. She dived in neatly, alongside the muddy

146

spiral of water, to find it numbingly cold and dark, but she was a splendid swimmer, and even hampered as she was by her clothes, she located the bag almost at once, although it was already sinking into the thick mud on the canal's bottom and it took several precious seconds to free it, but she hauled it loose and gained the surface, thankful to find the bank so near. But she still had to reach it and she would have to hold the bag above water—no easy task, for the cats inside were struggling to free themselves, half drowned though they were. She trod water, the bag balanced precariously on a shoulder, but what with cats and cold she was half drowning herself by now, so that Taro's dive to bring him up beside her went unnoticed until his voice, very matter-of-fact, said in her ear: 'Give me the bag, my dear. Can you make it to the bank?'

She nodded; speech was impossible for the moment, her teeth were chattering too hard, but without the bag it was easier and she contrived to say: 'Butch…'

Taro was hauling her on to the bank with more speed than delicacy. 'Pieters is here, don't worry.' He added on a laugh, 'And Aunty, bless her!'

Alexandra scrambled untidily to her feet, her clothes clung, heavy with ice, muddy water and freely festooned with bits of weed. Her hair had come undone and was streaming in a dripping mass over her shoulders. The doctor put an arm round her shoulders and said pleasantly: 'The Witch of Endor in person. Come on.'

Aunty was standing with Pieters, and growling Butch stood between them facing Penny, but Miss Thrums turned at their approach. 'Safe and sound, I see,' she remarked cheerfully. 'Get Alexandra into her boots, Taro, and give me the bag, I'll go straight to the house with Nibbles and Kiki.'

She was given the bag and Taro said something to her, but Alexandra had no idea what it was, she was suddenly tired and giddy, brought to a standstill by fright and cold. She felt the doctor's arm tighten around her shoulders and leaned her sopping head gratefully against his wet shoulder, clinging on to him with both hands, just as though, now that the danger was over, she were indeed drowning. She could have stayed like that, wet and shivering with cold and utterly happy, for ever, but her companion's firm: 'Now, now, girl, much though I'm enjoying this little interlude, I think we should get back to the house,' brought her to her senses.

'Penny?' she asked.

He gestured briefly. Penny, with Pieters beside her, was ahead of them, being escorted back to the house. Taro took her arm and began striding ahead, taking her with him at a fine rate. 'Speed is the essence,' he said cheerfully, 'hot bath and a double whisky afterwards.' He glanced down at her and grinned. 'Two baths, perhaps.'

They went along the lane and through the gate once more and this time he paused to lock it. But now there would be no need to do that, for when they reached the hall there was a serious-looking young woman and a middle-aged man waiting for them. The doctor greeted them briefly and went across to speak to Penny, but he was back again in a moment to give Alexandra a friendly push in the direction of the stairs. 'Up with you,' he commanded. 'I'll send Nel up with the whisky, we'll talk later.'

But first she had to say good-bye to Penny; she mounted the stairs afterwards, dragging her wet cold feet a little, Penny's softly spoken words still in her ears. 'If ever I get the chance, I'll do you a bad turn,' she had said, and smiled brilliantly, and Alexandra had no doubt, given the opportunity, she would.

But a hot bath and freshly washed hair did a great deal towards putting things into their proper perspective. She put on the wool dress and did her face and hair and feeling a little peculiar from the whisky, went downstairs.

She went straight to the kitchen, knowing that there was the most likely place for the cats to be. They were lying before the warmth of the Aga, looking decidedly under the weather, though Miss Thrums, who was with them, assured her that the vet had been, pronounced them very little the worse for wear, given them suitable injections and gone off to the study with Taro to take a look at Butch. She bent to stroke Kiki. 'And you, my dear, you're none the worse, I hope—so brave—all that icy water, none of us can thank you enough.' She looked Alexandra over carefully. 'I must say that you look perfectly all right, and such a nice colour.'

'Whisky—but I feel fine, thank you.'

Miss Thrums took off her glasses and polished them. 'Penny has gone.' She put her glasses on again and looked at Alexandra through them. 'Just for a little while I was afraid that she was going to get her way.'

'Her way?' A stupid question when she knew the answer.

'Why, she wanted Taro, my dear, and more than that, she wanted his wealth and this house—not that she loved him; he could give her these things, though—silly of me not to realize it sooner and foolish of me to suppose, even for a moment, that she would succeed, but as one grows older I suppose one becomes more fanciful.'

'Then I must be very old indeed,' said Alexandra, 'because I had the same fancy, but unlike you, Miss Thrums, I was terrified that it would come true.' She smiled bleakly. 'I was so frightened…'

Miss Thrums smiled very kindly. 'My dear, it would be quite natural, in the circumstances, for you to feel like that.'

'Feel like what?' asked Taro from the door. He strolled towards them, cast a quick professional eye over the cats and then took a more leisurely survey of Alexandra. 'Feel like what?' he asked again, and he so obviously expected an answer that she said hastily: 'Oh, we were just talking…' and was rescued by Miss Thrums': 'We were talking about Penny, Taro—I think that we both felt that something wasn't quite right, but it's so hard to know just when.'

'What is to become of her?' asked Alexandra. 'Will she go to her parents?'

He shook his head. 'Her boy-friend, so she told me. She wasn't in the least sorry for trying to drown Butch and these two, you know, and she wouldn't tell me why she had done it, though I suspect that she wanted to get even with me. She needs treatment, of course, has needed it for years—long before she had the car crash.' He stirred Nibbles with a gentle toe. 'Shall we go to the sitting room and have a drink—I've asked Pieters to put dinner forward half an hour; I have to go out again this evening.' He looked at Alexandra. 'I'd like to talk to you before I go.' His eyes were intent on her. 'You're none the worse for your swim? What a difference a bath does make.'

She contrived a smile. 'I'm fine—the whisky was a bit strong.'

He laughed. 'It was meant to be. You're pretty good in the water, aren't you?'

She said with a complete lack of conceit: 'I can swim well—my brother taught me, but I was frightened.'

'So was I.'

'How did you know where we were? Oh, Miss Thrums, of course.'

'And Pieters—I was met by a mixed chorus, rendered, thank heaven, with such brisk clarity that I was on the bank only a few seconds after you had gone in—very long seconds, Alexandra.'

She coloured faintly and didn't answer and he said pleasantly: 'Well, how about that drink?' becoming all at once the genial host.

They had their coffee in the sitting-room, and Miss Thrums, making no bones about it, declared that they would want to have their little talk while she went to see how the cats were faring and confer with Pieters. The doctor closed the door behind her and came back to his chair, and Alexandra, wishing to take the bull by the horns, said at once:

'You would like me to leave, wouldn't you? I haven't a job here now, have I? but you don't have to feel awkward about giving me the sack—I shall go home and have that holiday I never got around to.' She didn't look at him. 'I've already put my things together, all I need is your advice as to how to get back.'

He didn't reply at once so that she glanced at him after a moment to find him smiling. 'Well, you won't get it, dear girl; I've other plans for your immediate future—if you would care to hear them?'

She nodded, her heart thumping uncomfortably, unbidden thoughts racing wildly around inside her head.

'A colleague of mine—I was talking to him this morning—is desperate for a nurse in the recovery room at his hospital in Rotterdam. There are several there, this one is the best—it would only be for a few weeks, filling a gap. Would you consider taking it—we'll see to the technicalities, all you will need to do is pack your bag and present yourself for duty.'

'When?' She forced her voice to sound businesslike.

'As soon as you like.' He gave her a slow smile. 'I shall miss you.'

She ignored the smile. 'I can be ready tomorrow morning.'

'Splendid. I'll run you down and hand you over, it's only twenty-five miles or so. Is eight o'clock too early?'

He couldn't get rid of her fast enough. She pushed the sad thought aside and said briskly: 'Of course not. It is only a temporary arrangement?'

'Yes, two or three weeks at the most, maybe less. The salary is quite good, you'll live in and no language problems, almost everyone you will work with will speak English of a sort.' His eyes searched her face. 'Alexandra, do you ever think of that fellow Ferris?'

She was so astounded that she could only gape at him. 'Anthony?' she managed at last. 'Good heavens, no—whatever made you ask that?'

He shrugged. 'Nothing in particular.' He had got to his feet as he spoke. 'I have to go—I'll see you at breakfast. Good night.'

She wished him a calm good night—it would be, she reflected unhappily, the last good night she was likely to exchange with him. He had got rid of her with an expertise which commanded her admiration while it surprised her too. She had hoped, now that she allowed herself to think about it, that he would have invited her to stay another day at least before she went back to England; she had actually begun to delude herself into thinking that he liked her, instead of which he was giving ample proof that he wanted her out of the way as soon as possible. A variety of wild ideas stirred in her brain; perhaps Penny hadn't gone back to England after all, perhaps he was even now on his way to see her, perhaps... She was interrupted by the return of Miss Thrums, who sat herself down with her knitting and wanted to know in a most ordinary voice at what time she would be leaving in the morning.

'You know,' exclaimed Alexandra, and added peevishly: 'If he told you why couldn't he have told me earlier?'

'Men take a long time to make up their minds,' remarked Miss Thrums obscurely, 'and once they have, no power on earth will alter them, however awkward it is for everyone else. He only told me before dinner, dear, and then it was because he wanted my advice as to whether you would be likely to accept.'

'Yes, but surely there was a Dutch nurse available? I could just as easily have left tomorrow morning and gone home.'

Her companion made a vague sound which could have meant anything, and went on: 'I daresay Taro thought you might like the opportunity of seeing something of Holland while you are here. There are some good shops in Rotterdam—not that it is my favourite city, I prefer The Hague. Amsterdam is beautiful too, but rather given over to modern youth, although there are still parts of it which are quite delightful. Perhaps you will have a chance to go to The Hague.' She rattled on, not giving Alexandra a chance to say a word. 'There are some tea-shops there—their cakes are delicious, although I have always thought that our English muffins and tea cakes cannot be bettered.'

Alexandra agreed, wondering how the conversation had got around to muffins. There were a lot of questions she would have liked to have asked, but it was a little difficult to drop them lightly between the tea cakes. And Miss Thrums showed no signs of abandoning her theme; Alexandra learned more about The Hague in the next ten minutes than at any time in her life, it was only when Miss Thrums paused and said quite unexpectedly: 'I was devoted to my sister,' that she realized that her companion had been talking largely for the sake of something to say. 'Taro's mother, you know,' said Miss Thrums. 'I spent a good deal of time here while she was alive. Taro still has his father, of course—I think you would like him—and he has his sisters. His father is visiting one of them at present, although normally he lives at De Kaag, which I expect you have discovered is quite near here. He has a charming house there now that he has retired; he is often here, too.' She put down her knitting. 'Taro was such a naughty little boy,' she mused, apropos of nothing. 'Shall we go to bed, my dear?'

Alexandra got down early to breakfast and so, to her surprise, did Miss Thrums. The doctor was already there, sitting at the table, going through his post. He got up as they joined him, inquired as to their night, reassured them as to the conditions of the household pets, enjoined Alexandra to make a good breakfast and then sat down again to finish his toast and coffee as well as his correspondence. When he had finished all three, he asked: 'Five minutes suit you?' and left them.

She stopped crumbling toast and put down her half full cup of coffee. She felt sick, not at the prospect of a new job, but at the idea of leaving the house and never seeing Taro again. She stared at her plate wishing she could tell Miss Thrums just how she felt. After a moment she said in a wooden voice: 'I've loved every minute of staying with you, Miss Thrums. You've been very kind, not just to Penny, but to me too, I'll never forget it—and your little cottage and the garden.' She sighed. 'It was a cobweb morning,' she went on, an incoherent remark which her hearer shouldn't have understood in the least, but she did.

'I know, my dear. Fairyland—it always is when the right person is with you. I've enjoyed having you; if I had married and had a daughter, I should have liked her to have been just like you. Now run along and put on your coat, Alexandra, you mustn't keep Taro waiting. I believe he has a lecture to give after he has handed you over.'

When Alexandra got down to the hall again, she found it very nicely filled; as well as Taro there was Aunty, Pieters, Nel and Bet the cook as well as the dear old man who pottered in the garden. She shook hands with them all, ending with Miss Thrums, who kissed her soundly and assured her that they were bound to meet again, sooner or later, and when she reached Taro's side, he said briskly: 'Shall we get started? We can leave our farewells for the moment, can't we?'

He ushered her outside, and if she had felt sentimental about leaving his matter-of-fact words cured her immediately. She got into the Rolls beside him and beyond a final wave to the little group of people standing in the porch, she sat like a statue. If he wanted to talk, she decided, thoroughly out of humour, let him begin the conversation. But apparently he didn't. They tore with silent power down the motorway and it wasn't until they reached the outskirts of The Hague, with barely fourteen miles to go, that he spoke.

'Have you enough money?' he asked her.

It was the last thing she had thought about; she had spent hardly any of her salary although in Rotterdam, being on her own, she might need to use a good deal more of it, even then, she had enough. She said, 'Yes, thank you,' and looked away, out of the window.

He didn't speak again until they were passing Delft; the town stood a little way off from the motorway, its spires and towers intriguing in the dull grey morning light. 'I suppose there's a good bus service?' she asked, thinking of days off to be filled.

'You would like to visit Delft? It is charming, although I prefer Leiden, naturally enough, I suppose. You liked it too?'

'What I saw of it appeared delightful.' She was stopped by his low laugh.

'My poor Miss Dobbs, how dull a life you have been forced to lead! You must do some sightseeing

before you go back home—you will be going to
your home?'

'I think so—I may look for a job first.'

'And where will you do that?'

'Oh, London.'

He had nothing to say to that but: 'There's the
hospital ahead of us.'

It was a modern building, very high and narrow,
set in the centre of a complexity of busy streets. It
seemed to Alexandra, watching the traffic racing
about like mad ants, that she would never dare ven-
ture from its door once she was inside.

The traffic appeared to hold no terrors for the
doctor. He cut through it skilfully, drew up before
the entrance and walked her inside. The hall was
large and reminded her forcibly of a railway station;
there were flower shops, newspaper kiosks, even a
small cafeteria in one corner. He marched her past
these, skirted an enormous internal telephone
switchboard, and started up the stone steps to the
next floor, where she was relieved to find he intended to take the lift.

'The sixth floor,' he mentioned casually, 'that is
where you will be working. Doctor Viske should
be there now.'

The lift stopped and he whisked her out and

across a large, wide-windowed vestibule, knocked on a door and ushered her in.

The man sitting at the desk was about the doctor's own age, but small and in comparison to his bulk, slight. He got up as they went in, greeted them in English, held a short conversation with Alexandra about her work, nodded pleasantly as if satisfied with her and said: 'If you would come on duty at midday?' He pressed a bell on his desk. 'Coffee first, though, then I'll get someone to show you where your room is and explain about the meals and so on. We do the shift system here—you'll be on duty until nine o'clock this evening, but the Hoofd Zuster will give you all the details.' He smiled at her. 'I hope you will be very happy while you're here, Miss Dobbs.'

The coffee came, and the two men, with a murmur of apology, lapsed into their own language briefly and then, as though to make up for it, plied her with questions as to her impressions of Holland. She answered them readily, but mindful of Miss Thrums' warning, suggested very soon that she should go and unpack and collect her uniform. Going down in the lift a few minutes later in the company of a big blonde, smiling nurse, she reflected that the parting she had been worrying about; making up speeches, deciding what she would say and trying to guess what Taro would say, hadn't been worth so much thought; it had been a matter of shaking his hand and wishing him good-bye—as simple as that, what else had been possible under the friendly eye of Doctor Viske? And Taro had shown no sign of regret, his smile had been cheerful, his farewells casually friendly. Probably he was glad to be rid of her, although there was no good in brooding over it. Alexandra gave herself a metaphorical shake and followed her guide up one passage and down another until they reached the nurses' home and her room.

Her case was already there, and the nurse, whose English was really very good, sat down in the small easy chair by the writing table under the window. 'I will stay,' she explained smilingly. 'If you will see to your clothes and put on the dress and cap?' she waved at these garments, laid out neatly on the narrow bed, 'and while you do this, I will tell you all.'

It was a splendid arrangement. By the time Alexandra had changed into the white uniform and perched the cap on her neat head, she was in possession of all the important points appertaining to life in the hospital. Very like home, she thought with a little pang of longing, and then told herself not to be silly; she would be in Rotterdam for such a short time, and it was a wonderful opportunity to see how they did things in a Dutch hospital.

Almost exactly as they did them in an English one, she had to confess a few hours later; save for the Dutch voices around her, she might have been at St Job's—the equipment was the same, the patients, once they were unconscious, were the same, the nurses did precisely the same as she did and all the doctors and surgeons spoke English, as did a great many of the nurses. She went off duty that evening, tired after a busy day, but knowing that there was nothing about her new job to make her nervous.

She was on duty at eight o'clock the following morning and would be free at half past four; before she slept she decided to take a look at Rotterdam— one of the staff nurses had offered to go with her and it would fill the evening nicely. She saw that life, for the time being at least, would be composed of activities with which to fill any free time she had, for that was the only way in which she was going to forget Taro.

The theatre block was busy the next day; she took her meals how and when she could in company with the other nurses, who grumbled good-naturedly about long hours and too much work and not enough money, so that she felt quite at home,

they advised her as to the best way to see Rotterdam, too. There was the Boymans' museum, they
told her, and a bus tour she could take through the
city with a guide aboard to tell her all about it as
they went, and a shopping precinct, a large one,
they enthused, where she could buy anything she
might want. And she must see the Town Hall, they
chorused, on the Coolsingel, one of the few buildings to have survived the bombing in 1940, and
after that the Bijenkorf, close by, one of the biggest
department stores.

She listened to them all; it was apparent that she
would have plenty to do while she was in Rotterdam and she was busy planning her evening as she
went back to work. She would have to go alone
after all, for the girl who had offered to accompany
her had had her off duty changed and wouldn't be
free. It didn't really matter, though, she had some
idea of the city now and once she found her way
to the Coolsingel she could get her bearings.

The streets looked crowded as she left the hospital, and the traffic seemed to be coming from
every direction. There was a pedestrian crossing
close by; she joined the crowd waiting impatiently
to get to the other side, and was swept along to the
opposite pavement. There was another road to cross
here and so many people by now that the traffic

island barely contained them. Alexandra warded off elbows, nudges and pushes and hoped that her boots would stand up to the trampling they were getting, but when an arm was tucked under her elbow, she felt that to be a bit much; she wriggled her arm to free it, and when nothing happened, put up her other hand to prise it loose. It was caught and held gently in a grip which made light of her tugs.

'Don't, dear girl,' said Taro from somewhere behind her. 'If I let you go now, I'll never find you again in this mob.' He was beside her now. 'Where are you going?'

'For a walk.' She was having difficulty with her breathing.

She heard his chuckle. 'Good lord, girl, in the rush hour in Rotterdam?' The crowd milling round them suddenly surged forward again, streaming away from them across the road, and another crowd, coming from the opposite direction, took its place. Taro turned her smartly round and regained the pavement she had just left and they were actually back again in the hospital forecourt before she said: 'Look, I've just come from here.'

'The car's here. Are you hungry?'

She was, but mere hunger wasn't going to weaken her; she had said good-bye to him once, she didn't want to go through all that again. 'I have my evening planned,' she told him firmly.

'Now that is a coincidence; so have I. There's a rather nice place where we can eat in Vlaardingen—the Delta, lovely views and good food.' He smiled down at her. 'The car's here.'

He ushered her into it with a swift ease which didn't allow her so much as a protesting breath, but she made one more try as he got in beside her. 'Look, Doctor van Dresselhuys, it's very kind of you, but we said good-bye yesterday…'

'Taro. I can't quite see what that has to do with it; I didn't say good-bye, even if you did, and I've only asked you out to a meal.'

He had eased the car into the traffic, sliding through it with practised skill. 'I'd like to hear what you think of the hospital—over dinner, and I've a message from Aunty. I was to be sure and tell you that she misses you—I think everyone misses you.'

She relaxed a little. 'And Butch—is he all right? And Nibbles and Kiki?'

'Going along nicely. Butch has a nasty bruise on one shoulder, from that bar, probably. He's making the most of it and getting very spoiled. The cats seem none the worse—thanks to you.' They were almost clear of Rotterdam and already in the out-

skirts of Schiedam. He went on: 'I made a few inquiries about Penny.'

That, she supposed, was to be expected. 'She's
all right?' she asked.

'She went to the boy-friend, I understand.
There'll be a certain amount of inquiries from the
police—she will have to make some sort of statement.'

They were almost in Vlaardingen, the towns
were so close together they might have been one.
'Did—did you speak to her?'

He threw her a sidelong glance. 'No, Alexandra,
I didn't.' He had turned off the main road and was
driving slowly towards the river. 'Here we are,' he
said, and parked the car. As they went into the restaurant she realized that he wasn't going to say any
more about Penny, not that evening, at any rate.

They went up to the bar on the fifth floor and
had a leisurely drink while they watched the boats
passing up and down the river below them, and
Alexandra regretted very much that she hadn't been
given the chance to dress up a little. She went away
to leave her tweed coat, casting a resigned look at
her skirted and sweatered reflection, and when she
rejoined Taro she said apologetically: 'I'm sorry
I'm not in the right clothes, but this was a bit unexpected.'

'You look very nice.' It was the kind of remark most men make, but he sounded as though he really meant it; she smiled, feeling more at ease because of it, and obediently studied the menu the waiter had offered her.

They dined superbly on smoked eel on toast, Steak Orloff, and then for Alexandra there was a rich confection of ice cream cunningly mixed with fruit and whipped cream, while Taro chose the cheese board. They sat a long time over their meal and even longer over their coffee, and Alexandra, well mellowed by the excellent hock Taro had chosen, forgot for the moment that she would probably not see him again once their evening was over, and enjoyed herself.

It was only on the way back that the hock lost its magic and she became more and more silent, so that Taro asked: 'Tired, Alexandra? Thoughtless of me to have kept you out of your bed so late.'

'I'm not tired,' she assured him hastily, 'and it's been a lovely evening.' She came to a halt there, unable to think of anything else to say. It had been a lovely evening, although she suspected that she had talked too much, not only about the hospital and her work, but about her home and her plans for the future, but at least she hadn't mentioned Penny once.

The eight miles or so to Rotterdam took only a few minutes, the hospital loomed before them, its shaded lights dimmed for the night. Taro stopped the car outside the main entrance and got out and opened her door, then walked with her to the nurses' home beside the hospital. At its door she paused and put out a hand. 'It was a lovely evening and thank you very much. Good-bye.'

He had her hand fast between his. 'Can you be ready by nine o'clock on Thursday?' he wanted to know.

'Thursday?' She blinked at him. 'That's my…' She stopped herself just in time from saying that it was her day off.

'Days off—Thursday and Friday, and I hope that you will spend them at my home, dear Miss Dobbs. I shall be in Leiden, of course, but Aunty particularly asked for you.'

The delight which had bubbled up inside her trickled slowly away; he was just being kind. For a moment she toyed with the idea of refusing his invitation, then remembered Miss Thrums, who was a dear old thing and would perhaps enjoy her company. 'How kind,' she said with careful coolness to make his eyes twinkle. 'I shall be glad to see Miss Thrums again.' She pulled her hand gently, but nothing happened, he still held it firm.

'I hope that you will be glad to see me again, too,' he said softly, and bent to kiss her. 'You may have your hand back now. Good night.'

Alexandra wasn't sure what she answered, it was to be hoped that it was something more coherent than her thoughts. She went quietly up the endless stairs to bed, undressing in a dreamlike world of excited thoughts. She would lie awake, she promised herself, and go over the evening very carefully, remembering everything he had said... She was asleep within five minutes.

CHAPTER EIGHT

THURSDAY was several days away; viewed in the light of an early morning in winter, as Alexandra dressed to go on duty, they seemed diuturnal, but once in the dining-room drinking her coffee and eating bread and butter and slices of cheese with the other girls, life took on a brighter aspect. Her companions were nice to her, chattering away in their school English, laughing at their mistakes and egging her on to have a go in their own language. It was a heavy morning in theatre too, and escorting patients from their wards to the anaesthetic room and then recovering them after the surgeons had finished their work gave her no time to ponder her own affairs. She was working as a staff nurse now, too, which made a nice change from her Sister's duties at St Job's.

The list went on steadily into the afternoon and they went in twos and threes to their dinners. It was half past four when Alexandra went off duty, and this time, with one of the other nurses acting as guide, she ventured out into the city. She found it a little modern for her taste and so unlike Leiden

171

that it seemed strange to think that two such different places could be so close to each other. But it was fun looking in the shop windows and comparing prices and then going to a modest little café for coffee.

'This is not a smart place,' explained Heleen, her companion, 'it is cheap, though, and the coffee is good. There are some splendid restaurants but they cost very much money—you have perhaps been to one such?'

'Well, I went to a very nice one yesterday, in Vlaardingen. It was called the Delta.'

Heleen's eyes sparkled. 'But that is a—a super place, most expensive. You were taken, of course.' She smiled. 'By Doctor van Dresselhuys, yes? We all know that you have been working for him. He is—how do you say?—the hero of all of us. So kind and charming; he is also very rich.'

It gave Alexandra a glow of pleasure to hear that, but all she said was: 'He can be quite sharp sometimes; he likes his own way, doesn't he?'

Heleen shrugged and laughed. 'But that is natural for a man, is it not? I would not mind how sharp he was if he took me out just once to a place like the Delta.' She leaned forward eagerly. 'Tell me, what did you eat?'

They took a bus back afterwards, in time to drink

yet more coffee with the late shift just off duty, and the next day Alexandra was on that shift herself. It was a duty no one liked; time for an extra sleep and a leisurely breakfast, certainly, but after that, once letters had been written or hair washed, no time at all, and being on duty at midday meant that one arrived at the tail end of the morning's list, with patients to take over while the earlier shift went to their dinners, before getting the recovery room ready for the afternoon cases. The day flew by and when she got off duty just after nine o'clock, she was too tired to do more than have a bath and fall into bed. The next day was better, though. She was on duty at nine in the morning and free at five o'clock, and the day after that was Thursday.

Alexandra was up early, to do her face and hair with extra care before making tea in the kitchen at the end of the passage. She had decided that she would be just a little late; over-eagerness wouldn't do at all. But at the last minute she couldn't do it; probably he had a heavy day's work before him and every minute would count. The carillon across the street was playing its tune for the hour as she went through the door, to find the Rolls outside with Taro at the wheel. Just for a few seconds she had the chance of studying his face, for he hadn't seen her, staring ahead of him, his profile grim, his brows drawn together, but when he turned his head and saw her the frown disappeared and his mouth relaxed in a smile.

He got out of the car and took her case from her hand and threw it on to the back seat before opening the door so that she might get in. 'Good girl,' he told her approvingly, as he got into his own seat. 'Thank heaven you're not one of those women who feel that they simply must be late.'

'Good morning,' she said demurely, 'and if I had been, would you have waited for me?'

'Now that's a question I must have time to answer.' He was driving without haste through the busy morning traffic. 'You look very nice,' he commented without looking at her.

She had to laugh. 'How could you possibly know? You haven't looked at me...well, only for a second...'

'Haven't I? You're wearing a tweed coat and one of those ridiculous wool hats—it suits you—and a mile and a half of scarf, leather boots and a shoulder bag. Your hair is all tucked away, which is a pity, and you came out of the door looking as though you were quite certain that I wouldn't be there.'

She turned to look at him, round-eyed. 'You can't have seen all that.'

'I did.' They were on the highway now, passing the Euromotel, and Delft's lovely skyline ahead of them seemed nearer than it was by reason of the cold, clear air. 'Do you read Robert Burns?' he asked.

'Me? No—hardly ever.' She thought about it for a moment. 'Why?'

'I can think of at least two of them which are appropriate to this conversation.' He slowed the car. 'Here's Delft.'

She was seething with curiosity about Robert Burns' poems, but she could see that he wasn't going to say anything else, so she looked out of the window and presently asked: 'Do you have to go away again as soon as we get to your home?'

'I'm afraid so, but only to Leiden. I'll be back soon after tea unless there's something unexpected to hold me up. I've private patients to see this morning and the hospital afterwards.'

'What about your lunch?'

She missed the gleam of amusement in his eyes. 'I'll get a sandwich.'

'That's not enough.'

He said on a half laugh: 'Do I detect a motherly concern for my welfare, Alexandra? The first, I swear.'

She bit back the swift denial on her tongue and

discovered at the same time a strong desire to burst into tears. Very silly, she told herself sternly. She would have to learn to control her feelings better than that and try and achieve the lighthearted, not quite friendly relationship which he seemed to prefer. She managed airily: 'Oh, I was thinking of your hospital patients; if you're hungry you'll be testy.'

'Good God, am I that? I had no idea.'

'Of course you're not,' she told him crossly. 'I was just saying…'

'I wasn't very nice to you when we first met, was I, Alexandra?'

It was so unexpected and she was so surprised that she could think of nothing to say. At length: 'Well, you were rather worried, weren't you? and you had no idea what I was like.'

He made a small sound and she wasn't sure if he had laughed or not, perhaps it would be a good idea to change the conversation. 'I wonder how Penny's getting on?' she asked, not really wanting to know, but he answered at once. 'I had a letter from her this morning, she appears to have landed on her feet under the doubtful protection of the boy-friend. She wanted to know if you were still here, and there was a message for you too—you were to remember what she said—does that make sense?' He didn't wait for her to answer. 'It was an interesting letter,' his voice had become bland with a hint of laughter in it. 'She told me that you—er—fancied me, Alexandra.'

She felt her cheeks grow warm and her pulse race and restrained herself only by a strong effort from shouting, 'But I do, I do,' at him. Instead she declared lightly: 'What a load of old rot, but Penny liked making little jokes.'

It was really rather annoying when he said cheerfully: 'What a pity! Being fancied—such a peculiar expression, too—might hold some delightful possibilities. Still, I've no time to worry about that now.'

They were driving down the lane which led to the house; a moment later they were there and less than five minutes after that he had gone again, with a nonchalant wave of the hand which left her feeling forlorn.

Upstairs, unpacking her bag, she decided that it was all her fault; she had drawn a modicum of comfort from Miss Thrums' pleased welcome and Pieters' smiling face, but why should she have expected more than pleasant hospitality from Taro? He had never—well, almost never, shown any desire to offer anything else, in fact, when she thought about it, his manner at times had been positively off-hand as though daring her to take him seriously.

She had been a fool to think otherwise; she should
have learned better by now. She slapped on some
more lipstick and went downstairs.

The day passed pleasantly. She and Miss Thrums
talked and walked and sauntered through the green-
houses and wasted agreeable time with the animals.
It wasn't until they were leaving the house for what
Miss Thrums called her post-prandial exercise that
Penny was mentioned.

'Taro had a letter this morning,' she observed as
they went across the garden and out through the
little gate opening on to the lane at the back of the
house. 'He would have told you, of course.'

Why of course? wondered Alexandra, and said
calmly: 'Yes, he did.'

'A strange letter. She is a clever girl, my dear,
and a cunning one. She wanted to know where your
home was, but Taro has no intention of telling her,
naturally; in a week or so she will have got over
her infatuation for him and forgotten all about you,
too. At present, though, you are a hated rival—you
know that.'

'Yes, but I can't think why—I've never given her
any cause…'

'Quite so, my dear,' said her companion briskly,
'but that would have made no difference to Penny;
she recognized you as a danger to her plans—I

doubt if she ever forgives you. But even if she had planned some small mischief she would have been unable to carry it out with you here, and by the time you return to England the urge to do so will have died a natural death.'

Alexandra stopped to stare at Miss Thrums. 'Is that why I was offered this job? To keep me here?...so that I wouldn't go back...' She paused quite speechless.

Her companion smiled. 'Well, I believe that was one of the reasons that Taro was anxious to go to the hospital in Rotterdam—besides, it has given you a chance to see something more of Holland, although as I told you, I don't care for Rotterdam.'

'No, I don't think I do either.' They were walking on again. 'It was kind of Taro to think of that— it never entered my head.'

Miss Thrums smiled again but offered no reply, merely observing that since they had arrived at the village it might be a good idea to visit its one shop and see if the sewing needles she required were obtainable there.

Their errand discharged, they turned for home. The afternoon was already darkening, with a mean, cold wind blowing in their faces.

'An unpleasant climate in the winter months,' commented Miss Thrums, 'and yet I like it.' As she closed the garden gate behind them, she asked: 'You like Holland, Alexandra?'

'Yes, I do.' She pushed back the tendrils of hair blowing round her face. 'I feel at home here, but I expect that's because everyone I've met speaks English, and I like all the people I've met, too—and this house is lovely.'

'Quite beautiful, even at this time of year—you should see it in the summer, with all the doors and windows wide and Taro pottering in the garden…and meals out of doors; it's perfect. Taro's lonely, though.'

'He must have friends.'

'Oh, any number, but what he needs is a wife and children.' Miss Thrums opened a side door. 'Here we are, despite the wind. How I shall enjoy a cup of tea.'

They were still sitting over it, toasting themselves before the blazing fire, when Taro came in. 'Dear boy,' beamed his aunt, 'would you like fresh tea?'

'Pieters is bringing it, thanks.' He sat down opposite Alexandra and smiled at her. 'You've had a pleasant day, I hope?'

'Delightful, thank you—doing nothing is lovely; I'd quite forgotten how hard I worked at St Job's—it's just the same here. But I like being busy.'

The tea came, and they sat comfortably talking

about nothing in particular until Miss Thrums declared: 'I must go to my room and fetch my needlework; idleness is such a waste of time at my age.'

'Let me go,' said Alexandra, suddenly anxious not to be alone with the doctor.

'Aunty wants to go,' said Taro lazily, 'she thinks we might like to have a cosy talk together, don't you, my dear? Fetching her embroidery is just a blind.'

Alexandra sat looking at her feet, struggling to think of a clever answer to this piece of impertinence. She gave up after a moment or so and glanced up in time to see Miss Thrums already at the door Taro was holding open for her. It seemed a good opportunity to let him see that she wasn't as meek as all that, so she got up too, intent on going too. But much too late; Taro had closed it before she was half-way there, and all he did was to catch her by the arm and walk her back to the fire, dump her in her chair and resume his own seat.

'Dear girl,' he observed mildly, 'why this rush to run away?'

'I'm not running away. I—I...'

He smiled at her then, a tender smile which set her heart thudding against her ribs. 'You're a darling,' he said softly.

She was powerless to think sensibly when he looked at her like that. She said inanely: 'Oh, am I?' and smiled herself, and when he got out of his chair and came across to her and pulled her gently to her feet and kissed her it seemed only natural to kiss him back.

'This is exactly the kind of cosy talk Aunty had in mind,' he murmured into her hair. 'I've had it in mind myself for quite a while now.'

He bent to kiss her once more and at the same time the telephone rang. He finished the kiss without rushing it, said 'Blast,' very softly and released her to answer it. 'For you,' he told her, and sat down on the sofa while she picked up the receiver.

It was her older brother. She said, 'Hullo, Edmund,' in pleased surprise, and then warned by his hesitant voice: 'What's the matter? Is something wrong? Mother—Father?'

It was their mother, he told her, suffering, of all things, from measles. Not well at all, he said soberly into her ear, and was there any chance of her coming home soon—just for a while, things were a bit difficult.

'Mother? Measles?' repeated Alexandra, amazed; she couldn't remember her mother being ill. 'Is she very bad?'

'Well,' said Edmund carefully, 'she's very

spotty, and off colour, of course. There's an epidemic round here, so it's difficult to get the district nurse for more than half an hour now and again.' She heard him sigh and knew what he was thinking. Her father would be rushed off his feet, Edmund himself, a junior partner with a small surgery which served one or two outlying villages, would be just as rushed, and with Jeff in Bristol and Jim busy at the farm, life was difficult. True, there was a dear old woman who came in to clean, but nipping up and down stairs to attend to an invalid's wants, let alone cleaning the house and cooking, would be more than she could manage. She frowned and looked inquiringly at Taro, unashamedly listening to her end of the conversation.

He said at once: 'Of course you must go. Will tomorrow do? I'll fix things with the hospital and drive you to Schiphol—you should be able to get on a morning flight, and you'll be home by tea-time.' He gave her an encouraging nod. 'Tell him that.'

'You're sure it's all right?' she asked as she put the receiver down a few minutes later.

'Of course—I'll see about a seat on the plane,' and when that was settled he came and sat down again, not beside her on the sofa, but in the big wing chair on the other side of the hearth. There

was, she saw at once, to be no resumption of the
magic which had held them both enthralled only a
few minutes earlier. Indeed, for the rest of that evening he was the kind host, the thoughtful friend,
ready with suggestions for her journey and practical
sympathy. Only as they said good night did he mention that he would drive her to the airport in the
morning, and even then he had added to his aunt:
'I would suggest that you came along for the ride,
Aunty, but it will be rather early!'

Which remark left Alexandra to suppose that although he was going to drive her to Schiphol he
didn't much mind if he were alone with her or not.

They covered the twenty odd miles to Schiphol
in less than half an hour. Breakfast had been early,
but there had been no hint of haste about it. Pieters
had served the meal in his usual unhurried manner
and Taro might have had the whole day idle before
him, to judge from his leisurely behaviour. Alexandra, who hadn't slept well, was edgy—she could
miss the plane, her mother might be worse, and
over and above these, Taro had left her, as it were,
half-way between heaven and earth. If only he
would say something.

They were actually getting out of the car at Schiphol before he did. Until that moment he had talked
trivialities with a detached friendliness which she

had found singularly quelling, but now, with her case in his hand, he paused.

'This isn't quite what I had planned for today,' he told her, and there was a gleam in his eye which quickened her heartbeat. 'I moved heaven and earth to be free to spend it with you, and here I am, speeding you away at the earliest possible moment.'

He took her arm and walked her into the arrival hall, dealt with her luggage, and started for the exit leading to her flight. They had only five minutes, she saw with dismay, and even at that moment a disembodied voice urged passengers for the London flight to go aboard. She said like a child: 'Oh, Taro, I've got to go, it's all so quick...'

'That's the best way,' he told her. She felt his hands on her shoulders. 'Good-bye, Alexandra.'

His kiss was quick and hard before he pushed her gently towards the barrier. She found herself the other side of it, on the escalator, and turned round to wave, not believing that he had let her go like that. Wasn't he going to see her again? He had said nothing, as far as she knew he didn't even know her home address. She crossed the tarmac and climbed the steps into the plane, quite unaware of what she was doing. Perhaps he was glad; perhaps he felt relief that this had happened to prevent them getting too involved. Well, she for one was involved, and would be for the rest of her life. She looked out of the plane window, sucking the sweet the stewardess had offered her, and wished she was dead.

London, after the quiet countryside in Holland, didn't impress her as she waited in the queue for a taxi once she had reached the air terminal, and Waterloo Station was bleak and crowded and she had to queue again for her ticket. She had time to telephone her home before she joined the small group of people waiting to be allowed on to the platform for the West Country train. She would have liked a cup of tea, but she didn't like to chance missing her place. She opened the paperback she had brought with her and prepared to while away ten minutes or so.

She looked up startled when she heard her name. Anthony Ferris was standing a yard or so away from her, staring at her, as surprised as she was. After only the smallest hesitation he came forward. 'Alexandra!' he exclaimed. 'Fancy seeing you here! I thought you were with that girl...'

'She's better—quite recovered.' She really didn't want to talk to him, but she had to be polite. 'How are you, Anthony?'

He told her at some length; she had forgotten how full of himself he always was. She listened quietly, saying nothing, for there was no chance to speak, anyway. It was only when he had at last finished and asked what she was doing at the station that she said: 'I'm going on holiday—just for a week or two.'

'Down to Dorset? I could do with a few days off myself. Maybe I'll pop along and take you out, Alexandra, just for old times' sake.'

'I shan't have time,' she told him coolly, 'my mother's ill.'

'All the more reason why you should have a break—you could show me some of your local scenery.'

She had her mouth open to tell him that she had no wish to show him anything when the people around her surged forward, taking her with him. She heard his: 'So long, Alexandra,' above the din of the station, and heaved a relieved sigh. To have chanced upon him of all people, in a crowded place like Waterloo, amongst hundreds of people who were strangers to her, had been just her rotten luck; thank heaven she had been able to shake him off. She hurried down the long platform, happily unaware that among all those same strangers there had been someone who knew her very well: Penny, who had watched her meeting with Anthony with the greatest possible interest.

Her father met her at Dorchester, and although he looked tired he gave her a great hug and said cheerfully: 'Mother's better—she's had a nasty chest, but it's clearing nicely—gave us all quite a fright. Of course she's tired and under the weather still, but now you're home perhaps she'll stop this silly nonsense about getting up to cook our meals. Mrs Petts has been managing—well, you know, opening tins and things, but you know what your mother's like, lying there fretting because she can smell something burning.'

'Poor Father—you really should have let me know sooner, I'd have come at once, for I've only been filling in time with this job Doctor van Dresselhuys found.'

They were driving out of the town through the rather bleak afternoon.

'So I imagined; your mother seemed to think otherwise—said on no account were you to be sent for.'

'She knows I'm coming?'

'I told her just before I came to fetch you.' Her father chuckled. 'She was a little put out, though I know she's very relieved and happy.'

'I'm glad—I can stay just as long as you want me to.'

Her father didn't look at her as he asked: 'Nothing lined up, my dear?'

'Nothing,' said Alexandra.

Her mother was sitting up in bed, thickly covered with spots and inclined to be tearful. 'Of all the nonsense,' she declared a little damply, 'bringing you back from that marvellous job—I'm perfectly all right.' She smiled through her tears. 'But it's lovely to see you, darling.'

Alexandra had cast off her outdoor things and was hanging over the foot of the bed, surveying her parent. 'It's lovely to be home,' she said resolutely, 'and that marvellous job was only going to last another week at the most—I was only filling in, you know, until the new staff nurse arrived.'

Her mother peered at her from under puffy lids. 'Are you going to see Doctor van Dresselhuys again?'

'Most unlikely,' said Alexandra, and felt a pang of sorrow shoot through her. 'We said good-bye this morning; he kindly drove me to Schiphol.' It was an effort to smile, but she managed it very well. 'I'm going to get your tea and get something for Father before surgery, then I'll unpack and rustle up some supper. How's the appetite, darling?'

Her mother shuddered. 'Food!' she exclaimed weakly. 'I can't face it.'

'You wait until you see what I'll concoct for your supper,' declared Alexandra. She tidied the bed and did the pillows and sat her mother comfortably against them. 'And while it's cooking we'll have a nice gossip.'

And so the next few days passed, with Alexandra cudgelling her brains over dainty little dishes with which to tempt her mother's appetite, while she prepared vast, satisfying meals for her father and Jim. What with that, and keeping the house just so with Mrs Petts' cheerful, rather muddled help, she had very little time to herself. Mrs Dobbs wasn't allowed to read; her eyes had been affected by the measles and she was forced to rest them, which meant that Alexandra spent all of her leisure sitting with her. The spots were hardening now and the invalid's chest was clear once more, and as there seemed no danger of further complications, she was sitting out of bed for an hour or two each day; it was just a question of time now, while she got back her strength; she was already longing to get back to her normal way of life and declared to any member of the family who would listen to her that she wouldn't be quite well until she did so. All the same, Alexandra nursed her carefully, pointing out, quite truthfully, that she couldn't possibly be seen by anyone until the spots had faded.

She was getting a little tired herself now; her days were long and busy, and there was little time for walking or riding, and the weather had changed too; there was snow on the ground and taking out the car had become a necessity rather than a pleasure. The village was largely cut off from the surrounding countryside, too, so that even their friends found it difficult to call. She cooked and baked and washed and ironed and read the papers more thoroughly than she had ever done before in her life, and when her father remembered to bring her a nursing journal from the village, she began to look for a job. She applied for several, although none of them really appealed to her, but she would have to do something; her mother was getting better now and she couldn't stay home for ever. She wrote her letters of application, gave them to the postman and then forgot them, not really caring if she had replies or not. The idea of working in London didn't appeal to her any more, but she knew that she wouldn't be able to settle in a small provincial hospital. Perhaps to go abroad would be the answer; she found the journal again and searched its advertisements once more. There were several: Australia, Central Africa, New Zealand…she wrote to them all.

She had been home for more than a week when Anthony turned up. She had gone to the door thinking it was a tradesman or someone wanting the doctor urgently, and stood, her mouth slightly open, looking at him in amazement.

'Surprised you?' he wanted to know with a smile which she decided privately was nothing short of self-satisfied. 'Told you I'd come and cheer you up—you look as though you could do with it, too.' His gaze travelled over her thick sweater and slacks and her hair, tied back from a face lacking make-up. 'Aren't you going to ask me in?'

She stood aside and he passed her to stand in the flagstoned passage, looking about him with an air of faint derision which annoyed her very much. She had left the back door open and the wind eddied about them so that he said impatiently: 'Good lord, is it always as cold as this? You must be frozen.'

She went to shut the door before asking in as civil a voice as possible: 'Why have you come, Anthony?'

'I told you—to cheer you up.'

'How kind, but I don't need it, thank you. My mother has been ill, I told you that, and she still isn't well; I'm busy all day and quite happy and very content.' She ushered him into the sitting-room and he stood and looked at its rather shabby pleasantness with that same air of derision before going over to the fire to warm his hands.

'I expect you'd like a cup of coffee?' she asked, still very civil.

'Rather—I'm hoping you'll ask me to lunch at the very least.'

She hesitated; her father and Jim would both be in for a meal before the afternoon surgery, although Jim was often late back from the farm. She had a wholesome stew on the stove, enough and to spare for any stray visitor; it would be unpardonable to turn him away, however unwelcome he was, without offering him a meal. 'We shall be glad to have you to lunch,' she told him quietly, and went to get the coffee.

When she returned with the tray, he had taken off his coat and made himself quite at home in her father's chair, moreover, he was at pains to make himself pleasant. They drank their coffee with a little spate of conversation before Alexandra excused herself. 'I must take my mother's morning drink up to her,' she explained, 'she sits out for a little while before lunch. Please help yourself to more coffee if you want it.'

Her mother was hanging over the banisters at the top of the stairs, her face, still spotty, but now more cheerful, alight with curiosity.

'Who's downstairs?' she wanted to know as Alexandra drew her back into her bedroom. 'Is it that nice doctor?'

Alexandra surveyed her romantic, hopeful mother with an almost motherly smile. 'No, dear, far worse than that—it's Anthony Ferris.'

Her mother accepted her Horlicks, made a face at it and said: 'But I thought you'd quarrelled.'

'We did. I can't think what's come over him; I met him, quite by chance at Waterloo when I was coming home, and he said something about coming down to see me, but I never imagined that he meant it.' She sighed. 'Mother, he's asked himself to lunch and he's downstairs, being pompous—how can I get rid of him?'

Her parent thought for a moment. 'If he doesn't go soon after lunch, I'll feel poorly and demand that you come up here—how's that for an idea?'

'Not bad. Supposing he doesn't take the hint?'

'Get your father on to him,' suggested her mother darkly, and they both giggled. Her father had a way with people he didn't like…

She went downstairs again presently, spent ten minutes in more polite conversation and then excused herself once more on the plea of getting the lunch. There was actually nothing to do; everything was cooking just as it should be and the upside-down pudding she had made earlier was steaming nicely in its saucepan. She sat on the kitchen table eating an apple, and wondered how long she could stay there without appearing rude.

In the end she had to go; the table had to be laid, and since they had a guest, it would have to be in the dining-room instead of the warm, cosy kitchen. She collected plates and put them to warm and went along to lay the cloth. But that small task couldn't be made to last for ever, she fetched her father's sherry and some glasses and went back into the sitting-room. Anthony was still sitting by the fire, reading *The Times*. He looked up as she went in, cast the paper down in the untidiest fashion and said: 'Oh, there you are. I must say, you're not being very friendly.' He sounded aggrieved.

'Well, we aren't very friendly in the first place,' Alexandra pointed out, 'and in the second I did warn you that I was busy—you are, after all, unexpected.' She dumped the drinks down on the table. 'I must just go and try the potatoes,' she said, 'do pour yourself a drink.'

She was in the kitchen when she heard the front door bell again. It was rung with some vigour and at length, and she wondered whom it might be—not another visitor, she thought gloomily and went to open the door. But Anthony had bestirred himself; the door was opened already and he was holding it wide so that Taro might enter.

CHAPTER NINE

THE doctor stood in the hall, towering over Anthony and ignoring him completely, staring at her. He was dressed, Alexandra noticed with the sharp eye of love, in impeccable good taste; his car coat open over a dark suit; he looked exactly what he was, a successful, wealthy man, who had never worn elderly tweeds in his life and would rather have died than driven a Morris 1000. She smiled gloriously at him and said in a voice quavering with delight, 'Hullo,' and only then realized that he was furiously angry. His crushing: 'Good morning, Miss Dobbs,' acted like a bucket of cold water over her and sent her soaring spirits down to zero, but she went on gamely: 'What a surprise!'

'So I can see for myself.' The subdued thunder of his voice made her jump. 'Penny was right.'

'Penny? Right?' she echoed feebly.

'You're not usually at a loss for words,' he informed her blandly.

She recovered sufficiently to say: 'Well, I'm not usually taken by surprise like this.'

'Evidently.' The conversation was hardly making

progress. He grunted and his irate eyes fastened upon Anthony. 'Are you staying here—er Ferris, isn't it?'

Anthony gave him a cautious look and said guardedly: 'Well, as a matter of fact, that was the idea.'

It was all that was needed for Alexandra to give way to bad temper.

'Was it indeed?' she wanted to know indignantly. 'Of all the…' she flashed a fiery glance at Taro. 'And what's all this about Penny?'

Before he could answer, her mother's voice, nicely modulated and quivering with curiosity, floated down from the upstairs landing. 'Alexandra dear, if we have visitors, would it not be a good idea to take them into the sitting-room? It might be warmer.'

Her daughter went pink. She called: 'Yes, Mother,' obediently and said to the two gentlemen looking at her: 'Well, since you're here, we might as well go inside,' and pushed open the door. 'And do take off your coat,' she begged the doctor with a kind of outraged hospitality which caused a reluctant gleam to appear in his eyes.

Anthony took a nervous drink of his sherry and sat down. He jumped up again at once because Alexandra was standing by the table and the doctor, despite his ill-humour, had the good manners to stand with her.

She poured out two glasses of sherry with a trembling hand and offering him one, said: 'Oh, sit down, do,' in a voice a little sharp by reason of her agitation and sat down herself. 'Now perhaps you'll explain,' she invited. 'I should like…'

She was given no chance of finishing, though. The doctor, sitting in her father's armchair, and reminding her forcibly of one of the more majestic Olympians, cut her short with a suave: 'You two met at Waterloo Station.'

She looked at him in bewilderment and said the wrong thing. 'However did you find that out?' she asked.

He took a sip of sherry and crossed one long leg over the other. If she hadn't known him better she might have thought, mistakenly, that he was enjoying himself. He said very evenly: 'Do you remember the last time we talked, Alexandra?'

Of course she remembered. She looked at Anthony with a heightened colour before she said yes.

Taro studied her pink cheeks. 'Then you will understand that I am a little…' he paused, 'surprised.' He was staring at her very hard. 'That you should rush back to England to rendezvous with…' he paused again and turned to look at Anthony rather in the manner of one who was surprised to find him still there. 'What was the name again?' he asked politely, and when Anthony mumbled 'Ferris,' said: 'Ah, yes, my regrettable memory.'

'There's nothing wrong with your memory,' said Alexandra tartly.

'Absolutely nothing,' he agreed smoothly, 'though I can hardly say the same for you, Miss Dobbs, but perhaps our last meeting meant so little to you that you had no cause to remember it.' He gave her a nasty smile and turned his attention to Anthony. 'And are you on holiday?' he wanted to know, and his manner was very much that of a consultant putting a student at his ease.

'Yes—no, that is, I had this idea...coming to see Alexandra—thought she might need cheering up and so on. We're old friends, you know?'

Taro's eyebrows rose gently. 'Indeed?'

Alexandra had finished her sherry and its gentle glow on her empty stomach was giving her a quite reckless courage. 'Look,' she said quite crossly, 'I'm tired of this—walking in here, asking questions—and I still want to know what Penny has to do with it—and why are you here?' She was looking at Taro, having quite forgotten Anthony.

The doctor stood up, putting her at a great disadvantage because she was forced to crane her neck to see his face. He said mildly: 'You know, I had thought that I had been given the right to ask questions of you, Alexandra.' He was leaning against the table, his hands in his pockets. 'I came because I had a letter from Penny, telling me that she had seen you and a young man, apparently on the best of good terms, surrounded by luggage, waiting to board a train together. I didn't believe her, but I had to come and see for myself; if it had been possible I would have come to England there and then.' His eyes searched her face. 'Perhaps you find that difficult to understand.' He sighed. 'It seems that just for once, she was writing the truth.'

'You could have written,' she began.

'Oh, I did,' he gave a short laugh, 'a dozen letters, and tore each of them up, for how does one write the things I wished to say, and to telephone is even worse. I decided to wait until I could come and see you—you must have known that I would do that.' He gave her a small mocking smile which sent a nasty shiver down her spine. 'Or was I utterly and completely mistaken?'

She cast a look at Anthony, who should have had the good sense to leave them to themselves but was sitting there, gaping. 'Oh, heavens above,' she cried, quite exasperated, 'Taro...' She got no further as the front door slammed and a moment later

her father came in. There was nothing to do but
introduce the two men to her astonished parent,
murmur incoherently, pour him some sherry and in-
vite Taro to lunch. She took a quick look at him as
she did so and was shattered by the look on his
face; it was cold and horribly polite and was smiling a nasty little smile which shrivelled her inside.
He refused with good manners as cold as his expression, chatted to her father for a minute or two
and then declared that he must be going, begging
her on no account to leave the warmth of the fire
in order to see him out. She didn't even say good-
bye, merely stood there, a look of such frozen mis-
ery on her face that Anthony asked: 'I say, old girl,
are you all right? A bit pasty-faced, aren't you?'

She rounded on him. 'I am not your old girl! The
nerve of it...and I never felt better in my life. Sit
down and be quiet; I'm going to see about lunch,
and when you've eaten it, I hope you'll go away,
for I never want to see you again!'

She flounced out of the room and banged the
kitchen door shut, to emerge five minutes later with
the stew, which she sat before her father as soon as
he and his guest had seated themselves at table.

'I'll take Mother's up,' she said in a voice
slightly louder than usual. 'Don't wait for me, will
you? I want to make sure that she eats it. I'll have

something with Jim when he comes in.' She gave her father a speaking glance. 'I'm not hungry.'

An explanation to which her father listened in some surprise; Mrs Dobbs was eating very well, she certainly needed no encouragement, and for his daughter to declare that she wasn't hungry was so unusual that he realized that something or someone had upset her badly. Not the young man at present bearing him company, he was sure of that, more likely that Dutch chap, to whom he had taken an instant liking. He replied with fatherly diplomacy, told her not to hurry herself on their account and addressed himself to the task of making conversation with the young man his dear daughter had foisted upon him. He served the stew and put a few leading questions, sufficient to start Anthony off on a self-satisfied eulogy of himself, which left Doctor Dobbs in the happy position of being able to think his own thoughts while making an occasional comment.

Mrs Petts brought in the upside-down pudding and then shuffled back presently with their coffee, which Doctor Dobbs swallowed hastily, with the comment that he had an afternoon surgery and would have to get started on it. 'Measles, you know,' he told his companion, 'quite an epidemic— we've had our hands full—still have. Sorry I can't spare the time to stay for a chat.' He rose from his chair. 'Alexandra won't be down for some time; she gets her mother back to bed for a rest about now and stays upstairs to read to her. Shall I say your good-byes for you?'

And Anthony was only too glad to agree; Alexandra hadn't minced matters with him; it was extraordinary, but she really didn't seem to like him—she hadn't seemed to like that Dutchman either, although there was a doubt at the back of his mind about that. He took his leave, already thinking rather smugly of the new Casualty Sister at St Job's—not a pretty girl, couldn't hold a candle to Alexandra, but she thought him pretty super. He got into his car and drove back on to the main road; if he went up to Yeovil he could get on to the London road and be in London in time to take her out for the evening—a little dinner, perhaps, nothing too expensive; he had his future, his brilliant future, to consider.

Doctor Dobbs took the stairs two at a time and entered his wife's bedroom circumspectly, not sure how he would find his daughter. She was sitting by the window, reading aloud from the woman's page of the *Telegraph*, her voice so very bright and cheerful that he looked warily at her and then cocked a silent eyebrow at his wife, who gave him a warning look before wanting to know if their guest had gone.

'Yes—he wanted to get back to London,' said the doctor vaguely. 'Funny sort of chap, full of himself, too—never had such a dreary meal. I wish that other—what's his name?—could have stayed, I liked him. He had to go back to Holland, he told me. I asked him if he wouldn't like an hour or two's rest first, but he seemed to think nothing of it. Nice car, too.' He cast a stealthy glance at Alexandra and turned his attention once more to his wife. 'A Rolls.' He strolled to the window and looked out. 'I thought you said he was a struggling GP, Alexandra?'

Her voice was wooden. 'I thought he was. It wasn't until we were in Holland...he's something big in anaesthetics, I believe—he seems to travel around quite a bit.'

'Does he now? Ah, well, you'll probably meet him again.'

Alexandra got up, casting the newspaper down in an untidy muddle on the floor, and made for the door. 'No, I shan't,' she exclaimed forcefully, 'not ever again!'

Her parents listened to her hurtling downstairs and the subsequent slam of the kitchen door. 'What happened?' asked Doctor Dobbs.

His wife shook her head. 'I don't know. I heard them—not that other silly fellow, but Alexandra and the Dutchman, they sounded as though they were having a nice healthy row, and then you walked in, my dear. Not that it would have made much difference, I imagine. Has he really gone? I mean, back to Holland?'

'Oh, yes. He told me that he was very glad to have met me, and asked me to convey his respects to you—those were his very words.'

Mrs Dobbs smiled slowly. 'How nice—old-fashioned, but nice. He'll keep Alexandra in order,' she added in a tone of satisfaction.

Her husband smiled at her tolerantly. 'My dear love, you heard what she said—they're not going to meet again.'

'Oh, pooh,' said Mrs Dobbs, looking very like her daughter. 'I feel much better, you know. I shall start pottering tomorrow.'

She gave her husband an innocent look which caused him to say at once: 'Now look, darling, there's nothing you can do.'

'Why, I shouldn't dream of such a thing,' she replied meekly.

She was as good as her word: within the next few days she gently but inexorably took back the reins of the household into her own hands, so that

Alexandra found herself with almost nothing to do and reluctantly sat down to fill in the various forms she had been sent in reply to her inquiries concerning a job. There was one, in Western Australia, which seemed to match her unhappy mood exactly. She was putting a stamp on the envelope when she heard a car draw up outside the house and despite herself, went to the window to see who it was. Hope, she had discovered during the last few unhappy days, dies hard.

It was the Morris 1000, with Miss Thrums, looking exactly the same as she always did, at the wheel.

Alexandra flung open the door as she came up the path and ran to meet her. 'Oh, how very nice to see you,' she cried, and meant it. Wasn't this Taro's aunt, someone who had surely seen him recently. 'I never thought we'd meet again. Are you on holiday? Can you spend the night? Mother and Father would love you to stay, I know. Come in.'

Miss Thrums beamed at her, her sharp eyes taking in the white, tired face.

'Dear child, how nice to see you again, too, and I shall be delighted to meet your parents.' She allowed herself to be ushered into the house and thence to the sitting-room where Mrs Dobbs was dozing before the fire. But she was instantly awake when she heard who the visitor was; Alexandra left the two ladies, surprisingly at ease with each other, and went to put the kettle on.

It was early for tea, but the afternoon was grey and cold and she had made some scones that morning; she carried in the tray and set it down beside her mother's chair, dispensed the tea-cups and the scones and went to sit on the floor by the fire.

'I was telling your mother,' began Miss Thrums, 'that I have come to ask a favour of her. I could have written, but knowing that she had been so poorly I felt it right that I should first see for myself just how she was. I'm happy to find that her progress has been so rapid, for now I feel emboldened to ask if I might take you back with me, Alexandra—just for a short time. I don't know what your plans are for the future, but I imagine that you might spare a week—that is if you would like to come? I've only been back from Holland for a few days, you know, and I find myself very lonely. I thought you would cheer me up if you could bear with my company—while you're waiting for a job.'

Alexandra put down her tea-cup. Miss Thrums did indeed sound lonely, but she had to be sure of something first. 'You're quite alone, Miss Thrums?' she asked, carefully nonchalant.

'Quite alone, child. I drove the Morris back on

my own this time. Taro has been so very busy—
here, there and everywhere, almost never at home—
I hardly liked to suggest that he should come back
with me.' She looked at Mrs Dobbs. 'My nephew
lectures a lot—all over the place.' She looked
vague. 'Germany, I believe, or was it Austria, this
time?'

It was Mrs Dobbs who spoke. 'Alexandra hasn't
had much fun here,' she observed, 'running the
house and cooking and cleaning and looking after
me.'

'You might go doing too much if I went,' said
Alexandra. Her voice was wistful although she
didn't know it; if Taro was so far away, just to be
with Miss Thrums, who loved him, would be better
than nothing.

'I promise you I won't, love.'

Alexandra got up to cut the cake. 'I'd love to
come, Miss Thrums—just for a week or so until
you've stopped feeling lonely; it will be a week or
two before I hear from the different hospitals I've
applied to. When do you want me to come?'

Miss Thrums was looking down at her plate so
that the little smile on her face went unseen. 'How
about coming back with me?'

'That would be fine—but not today, surely?'

'Of course not,' protested her mother. 'You'll

stay the night, Miss Thrums, my husband will be delighted to meet you—you could go tomorrow morning, perhaps?'

The two older ladies agreed on this before returning to their tea and pleasant small talk which held no word of Taro, and presently Alexandra went away to make up the bed in one of the guest rooms, bearing the tea-tray with her, and only when her footsteps had died away down the passage did Mrs Dobbs say with deep satisfaction: 'You have no idea how delighted I am that you've come, Miss Thrums. There are one or two things I should like to know…'

They left the next morning with Alexandra driving, for as Miss Thrums so sensibly remarked, she was by far the better driver of the two of them, especially on the motorway. 'We can get as far as Basingstoke and take the Reading road,' she explained, 'and then go through High Wycombe and Hemel Hempstead, then I can drive, for I shall be on familiar ground then.'

They did as she suggested, stopping for lunch at a small village inn and then pressing on. Miss Thrums was a good driver although surprisingly reckless at times, and Alexandra, who wasn't at all bad herself, was surprised at the speed at which they travelled, probably due, she told herself, to Miss Thrums' whimsical habit of talking to her motorcar.

'You must forgive me, my dear,' said that lady, disconcertingly reading her thoughts, 'but the elderly are allowed to be a little eccentric, you know. Taro always refers to my peculiarities as my venerable foibles, which makes them sound quite normal, doesn't it?'

Alexandra laughed and her companion said instantly: 'Ah—how nice to hear you laugh, child. You have become very serious since I last saw you. Probably you have been anxious about your mother.'

'Yes, Miss Thrums.'

'A nasty infection, measles, especially when one is older.' She went on as though she hadn't changed the subject: 'I wonder if Taro found Penny?'

'Found Penny?' Alexandra heard her voice falter although she tried to keep it steady. 'Why?'

'He wished to make it quite clear to her that she was wasting her time—and everyone else's—by trying to make trouble for other people. He intended to suggest, I believe, that she should remove herself to some remote part of the world where she would have no chance to make a nuisance of herself.'

'He can't do that—besides, he did believe her, but...'

She wasn't allowed to continue. 'Why, here we are, almost home,' interrupted Miss Thrums. 'I'll drop you off and go on to collect Sambo and Rover. Will you put the kettle on, my dear, and we will have a little meal and a nice chat.'

So Alexandra had to contain her patience until the fire had been lighted, the table set before it and laid with what her hostess called high tea, and only when the animals had been fed did they sit themselves down cosily one each side of the bright fire and then it was that Miss Thrums went on, just as though she had never stopped: 'Of course Taro didn't believe her, Alexandra—no man with his wits about him would have done so. Remember her history and the circumstances leading up to her return to England. Granted, he was as enraged as any man might be on hearing that the girl he loved had been seen only hours after she had taken leave of him, apparently about to take a trip with another man—but if he had stopped to think…but of course he was far too angry for that, and to make matters worse, he was quite unable to go and find out for himself—work, you know. It was a great pity that he should meet that young man. I heard all about it.' She paused to pour second cups. 'Two such un-

pleasant days, during which he was unendingly
civil and addressed me as Aunt Euphemia, ate almost nothing and flung himself into his work with
quite unnecessary vigour. I told him on the third
day that I intended to return home, and I am not
sure if he really heard me. True, he wished me
good-bye and said all the right things, but I don't
think that my departure made any impression on
him.'

Alexandra cracked a brown egg. 'Oh, he must
have known—he's very fond of you.'

'Yes, my dear—I know. He's very fond of you
too, although I believe that to be an understatement.'

Alexandra spooned her egg carefully, because
her hand was shaking a little. 'He's nothing of the
sort,' she declared strongly. 'He—he rushed in and
he was so nasty—you know what I mean; his mouth
was a thin line and he looked at me as though I
wasn't there, and he laughed...'

'He has a very nasty temper,' agreed Miss
Thrums in a soothing voice, 'although he seldom
loses control of it, and it has been my experience
that the angrier he is the more arrogant and cold he
becomes. His father has a nasty temper too, but my
sister could always calm him down—just as you
will with Taro, child.'

Alexandra choked over her bread and butter. 'Miss Thrums, you don't understand. He—he doesn't want to see me again—he just walked out. I did ask him to stay to lunch,' she explained like a hurt child. 'He was so dreadfully polite; if he'd sworn at me or shouted, I might have thought…though I had no reason to really.' She drank some tea and said in a tight voice: 'Would you mind if we don't talk about him?' She added in a more determined manner: 'I've written about a job in Western Australia—it sounds rather interesting.'

Miss Thrums might be elderly; she was wise too. She said at once: 'I was there for a while when I was a girl—a sheep station outside Perth, I was engaged to the man who owned it. A strange country, but wonderful too. I could have made it my home.'

'But you didn't?' Alexandra prompted gently.

'He was killed during the war—in Italy. I came back here and picked up the pieces of my life, and Taro's mother helped me. Taro was quite a little boy then, but we had a great affection for each other, even then. His sisters are nice people too, but Taro is my favourite.'

She took a slice of cake. 'I'm sorry, Alexandra, we weren't going to talk about him—you must forgive me.' She stretched her sensibly shod feet to the fire. 'What shall we do tomorrow?'

Their days were nicely filled; little shopping trips, walks with the dog, the rector to entertain to tea, books to fetch from the travelling library when it came to the village. And these small, restful pursuits soothed Alexandra. Her face was still without colour and there were shadows under her eyes, but she was cheerful again, at least in company, and if Miss Thrums, who had sharp ears, heard muffled sobs during the night, she took care not to mention the fact. But after a week, on the day that Alexandra had a letter asking her to go for an interview for the job in Australia, she was sent down to the village to fetch the eggs, and when she was safely out of the way Miss Thrums went to the sitting-room, sat down at her desk, and drew the telephone towards her.

It was cold and grey the next morning, as it had been for several days, but at least it wasn't raining, and the wind, although a snarling monster from the east, would be splendid for drying; Alexandra declared herself ready to do the washing and when Miss Thrums protested, pointed out that they might have to wait days for blue skies and sunshine, and taking a load into the washerette in Needham Market would mean hanging about for it—besides, she added in a wheedling tone, she felt like it. And Miss Thrums, recognizing the therapeutic benefits of hard work, gave in gracefully.

So Alexandra retired to the little washhouse attached to the kitchen, and began her self-imposed task. She emerged some time later, an old raincoat of Miss Thrums' tied round with string round her waist over her dress, her feet thrust into far too large Wellingtons. She had a basket of washing balanced between her arms and trod carefully across the garden to its end, where the clothes line stood. She wasn't happy, but having something to do made her feel better. She dumped the basket and started on the task of hanging the things out.

She had a neat row of flapping towels and a sheet in her hands when she looked up and saw Taro. He was standing quite close, so that she could see that he was wearing the shabby tweeds and a massive sheepskin jacket over them; she took in these details in a dream-like fashion and then closed her eyes, sure that she was only imagining something which she so much wanted to be true. The wind blew an extra strong gust just then, tearing her hair from its pins so that it spilled around her shoulders and covered her face. She pushed it impatiently out of her eyes and took another look. He was there all right, and even nearer now.

He said in a strong voice, because of the wind, 'My adorable Miss Dobbs,' and smiled at her, which so agitated her that she stammered a little. 'Don't call me that.'

He took another step towards her and took the wet sheet from her hands and flung it carelessly over the line, and deliberately misunderstanding her: 'Then I won't; I have never thought Miss Dobbs suited you—for my part I would prefer it to be changed to Mevrouw van Dresselhuys.'

The wind was blowing a gale now, bringing with it a few drops of icy rain; the sheet, so carelessly flung, flapped wildly off the line and on to the recently turned earth of the kitchen garden, where it lay, very muddy. Alexandra looked at it, dismissed it as unimportant and said quietly: 'I thought I would never see you again.'

If she had put out a hand, she could have touched him.

'How would that be possible, my darling, when I love you more than anything else in this world?' He pulled her into his arms, stroking the wet hair away from her face.

'I thought you loved Penny…' She spoke into the rough warmth of his jacket.

'Never, dear darling. I pitied her, of course, but did you not also pity her? And I felt amusement at her antics as she recovered, until a faint suspicion that she wasn't quite what we thought she was—nothing she said or did, not at first, just a warning bell in the back of my mind—and all the while I was thinking about you and not admitting it to myself. Even when I arranged for her to stay with Aunty I refused to acknowledge that I was doing it largely so that I might keep you close to me. Only on that morning—that cobweb morning, you remember?—I finally admitted that there was no one else for me—only you. I very nearly told you.'

'Oh, Taro, why didn't you? There was I waiting to fall into your arms like an apple off a tree...'

He kissed the top of her wet head. 'My darling, is not the expression an overripe plum? Though as you resemble neither, it can be of no consequence.' He laughed a little and tilted up her chin to kiss her, and neither of them noticed the rain, coming down in good earnest now.

'Why are you here?' asked Alexandra when she had her breath back.

'Aunty has been telephoning me each day—yesterday she told me that you were on the point of accepting a job in Western Australia; so I came at once.'

She thought for a minute, then asked a trifle peevishly: 'Why did you leave me alone so long? Why didn't you come sooner?'

He kissed her with such thoroughness that it really didn't matter if he answered her or not, but he did. 'Work, my dearest, work I couldn't leave for anyone else. When I went to your home I handed everything over to my registrar, but he could only manage for forty-eight hours. I had to go back—I ought never to have come, but I had to know even though I knew that Penny was lying.'

'You were furious,' she reminded him.

'Naturally—what further proof could you want of my love?'

It was a point she hadn't thought of and it struck her, standing there in the shelter of his arms, as most satisfactory. She sighed and smiled up at him.

'I must look a perfect fright,' she observed, and indeed she was by now very wet, her hair plastered round her ears. Miss Thrums' Burberry, although still stoutly waterproof, did nothing to improve her appearance either.

Taro studied her face. 'You're beautiful,' he told her, and she knew that he meant it, 'and you always will be.'

It seemed only kind to express her appreciation of this remark, but presently she asked: 'You don't have to go back at once, do you?'

'This evening—and you are coming with me, Alexandra, for we have to see about getting married as soon as possible—you'll come?'

'Yes, of course, Taro.'

He threw an arm round her shoulders and began to walk back to the cottage. The rain and wind, she saw, didn't bother him in the slightest—it didn't bother her either, she suspected that both of them secretly enjoyed that kind of weather. They would probably have a family of tough, healthy little boys who wouldn't mind wind or bad weather or muddy canals, just like their father. She chuckled at the thought and Taro stopped to look down at her. 'Why did you do that?' he wanted to know.

'Oh, I was just thinking. I'll tell you one day. It was something nice.'

A smile hovered round his mouth. 'I'm a patient man, but not all that patient.'

'Little boys in Wellington boots,' she told him seriously, and his smile widened into a grin as he picked her up and swung her round, then set her gently on her feet again to kiss her once more. Presently they went on again, the wind, quite ferocious now, bowling them along until they reached the kitchen door.

Alexandra took a last look at the grey, windswept landscape. 'What a lovely morning, Taro,' she observed in great content.

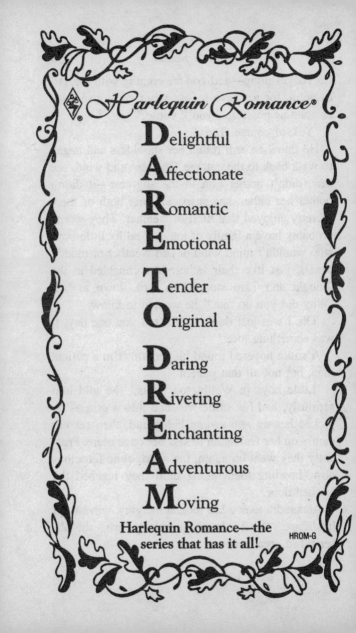

Harlequin Romance®

Delightful

Affectionate

Romantic

Emotional

Tender

Original

Daring

Riveting

Enchanting

Adventurous

Moving

Harlequin Romance—the
series that has it all!

HROM-G

HARLEQUIN PRESENTS

HARLEQUIN PRESENTS
men you won't be able to resist
falling in love with...

HARLEQUIN PRESENTS
women who have feelings
just like your own...

HARLEQUIN PRESENTS
powerful passion in
exotic international settings...

HARLEQUIN PRESENTS
intense, dramatic stories that will keep you
turning to the very last page...

HARLEQUIN PRESENTS
The world's bestselling romance series!

Harlequin® Historical

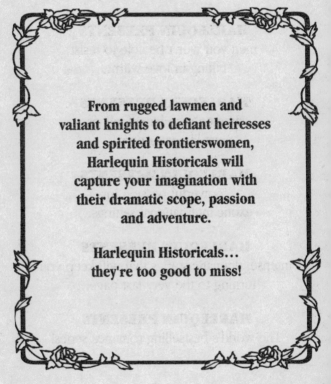

From rugged lawmen and
valiant knights to defiant heiresses
and spirited frontierswomen,
Harlequin Historicals will
capture your imagination with
their dramatic scope, passion
and adventure.

Harlequin Historicals...
they're too good to miss!

HARLEQUIN®

A M E R I C A N ◆ R O M A N C E®

LOOK FOR OUR FOUR FABULOUS MEN!

Each month some of today's bestselling authors bring
four new fabulous men to Harlequin American Romance.
Whether they're rebel ranchers, millionaire power brokers
or sexy single dads, they're all gallant princes—and
they're all ready to sweep you into lighthearted fantasies
and contemporary fairy tales where anything is possible
and where all your dreams come true!

You don't even have to make a wish…
Harlequin American Romance will grant your every desire!

Look for Harlequin American Romance
wherever Harlequin books are sold!